Bargain Haunter

ReGina Welling and Erin Lynn

Bargain Haunter

ISBN- 978- 1081770457

Cover design by: L. Vryhof

Interior design by: L. Vryhof

http://reginawelling.com

http://erinlynnwrites.com

First Edition

Printed in the U.S.A.

Contents

CHAPTER 1

The final peal of the bell signaling the end of services at Mooselick River Presbyterian still echoed over the town when Martha Tipton and a couple of her cronies marched down Lilac Street wearing their Sunday best. I, however, was wearing a pair of cutoff shorts and the skimpiest tank top I owned, in an attempt to stay cool in the early August humidity.

I stopped weeding a bed of dahlias to watch the advance with interest. Interest that quickly turned to dismay when Martha made eye contact, and the determined women turned in at my driveway.

Since it was too late to duck inside, I mustered up a smile.

"Good morning, Mrs. Tipton. Ladies. What can I do for you?" I offered drinks, which they declined and chairs in the shade of the porch, which they accepted without too many harsh looks at my attire.

Martha wasted no time getting right down to business. "As you probably know, the third annual town-wide yard sale is coming up the second week of July, and we were wondering if you might be willing to pitch in a few items for the church charity table. Last year, we donated four hundred dollars to feed the homeless."

"Still didn't top the Methodists, though, did we?" One of her friends muttered in a distinctly annoyed tone. "They raised five hundred dollars for cancer research."

I bit my lip to hold back a smile.

"Let it go, Patricia," Mrs. Tipton ordered from between clenched teeth. "It can't be helped now."

Patricia subsided, but not with any measure of grace. She smoothed the lapel of her pink suit, glared at Martha, and got the last word in before she clapped her lips closed.

"Easy for you to say. You're the one who got all cocky and said if we didn't raise the most money, none of the Methodists had to be on the committee this year."

To forestall a knock-down, drag-out church-lady fight on my front porch, I said, "I'm sure I can rustle up a few things for the sale. Anything to help a worthy cause." And that right there was where I made my fatal mistake.

"Anything?" The third lady, who wore a flowered dress, piped up with more excitement than I thought was warranted. "Would you be willing to join the organizing committee? It's time the next generation learned to pitch in and do their civic duty."

How bad could it be? In my former life, I'd put on gala events that raised millions, so helping with a yard sale shouldn't be much of a stretch.

"Sure. Tell me where and when, and I'll be there."

Flowered dress introduced herself. "Elizabeth Tate, but you can call me Bess. Everyone does. We're meeting at the town office next Wednesday at eleven o'clock. I'll look forward to seeing you then."

She shot me smile, and I'm sure I only imagined the canary feather sticking out of the corner of her mouth.

I watched them walk back the way they had come, then went inside for a glass of iced tea. My first thought when I heard the doorbell ring was that the yard sale brigade had returned. But when I peered through the wavy glass and recognized the attorney I should have engaged to represent me in my divorce, but didn't standing on my front porch, I kept her waiting longer than was polite.

"Patrea. I wasn't expecting ... how did you find me?" *Why* had she tracked me down was the more important question.

Patrea Heard tipped her head down to survey me from over the top of her glasses. "It wasn't difficult when your name was all over the news. Murder in Mooselick River. Film at eleven." As usual, her tone carried a heavy load of sarcasm.

"Oh." You'd think she was an alien the way I just stood there with my mouth open halfway.

Patrea finally had to give me a nudge. "Can I come in?"

I really was an idiot.

6

"Yes, I'm sorry. Of course. I'm just surprised to see you here." Mind racing to figure out what would lure Patrea out of the city, I swung the door wide to let her into the front hall.

"Can I get you anything? I have iced tea or coffee."

Eyes alight with curiosity as she looked around, she waved the suggestion away. "I'm fine. The architecture of this house is fabulous. That tower with the lightning rods." She fluttered a hand over her heart. "I bet you can see all over town from up there. And the bargeboard. So intricate and in really good condition."

I nodded, even though I had no idea what she was talking about.

"How many rooms?" she asked without giving me time to answer. "Just look at the mix of oak and walnut moldings. Tell me you're not planning to paint all this gorgeous trim." For emphasis, she grabbed my shoulders and gave me a little shake. This was not the Patrea I had come to know.

"No. No, I'm not. Someone already painted in the kitchen, though. What's bargeboard?" Every time I turned around, someone tossed out another term, I didn't understand.

At the mention of the painted kitchen, her expression alternated between appalled and fascinated."Where? Show me!"

All I could do was point the way, and she blasted past like a whirlwind to leave me standing in open-mouthed disbelief. I'd seen her advocate fiercely for causes she believed in, I'd seen her annoyed and even downright furious at injustice. I'd never seen Patrea passionately excited over a set of baseboards before. I found it weirdly disconcerting.

"Okay, well, this isn't so bad." When I caught up, I found her on her hands and knees inspecting a paint-flaked corner of the molding around the door. She poked at the chipped spot with a fingernail. "They didn't paint over premium wood. This is just pine. I'd say the kitchen was remodeled, and they were able to match the profiles but not the materials, so they painted the woodwork instead. The paint might be lead-based since the cabinets look to be pre-seventies. You'll want to have it properly remediated and sealed before you have babies."

"I'm not ... never mind." No one seemed to listen when I said I wasn't planning on marriage and a family. Not anymore.

I had to know. "Why are you here?"

"You didn't return my call." Patrea rose and smoothed a nearly invisible wrinkle from her slacks. Some women can wear linen and come off looking fresh as a daisy. I'm not one of them, but she was.

"We need to talk, but first, tell me how you ended up with this gorgeous house." Angling her head, she spotted the doorway to the living room and headed in that direction, leaving me no choice but to follow.

After she inspected the fireplace surround, we settled across from each other, and I launched into the story of how Mrs. Tipton, the town clerk, had talked me into buying Willowby House and everything in it for the back taxes.

"And you didn't even do a walk-through of the place first?"

"There wasn't time. The clock was ticking to get my bid in under the deadline as it was. I'm not normally so impulsive, but I'm glad I took the chance. It's a great house." Even if I still felt like it wasn't fully mine.

Her shrewd gaze roved around the room, and as she took in each piece of furniture, Patrea assessed.

"At the right auction, you could make back most of your investment from the pieces in this room alone. I wouldn't mind taking that occasional table off your hands."

"If it's only a table occasionally, what is it the rest of the time?"

"Funny," she said smirking. "What are you planning to do with the place?"

I sighed. "Why does everyone think I have to do something with it? One of my friends says I should open a bed and breakfast, or maybe turn these rooms into an antique shop. Everyone agrees it's too much house for one person."

"You don't?"

"I haven't had a lot of time to think about the future. Not while I'm still dealing with the matter of my past. Can I assume my ex is the reason you've decided to pay me a visit?" What other reason would she have? We were friendly, but not friends. "I told you I'm not interested in going after Paul's money. I'm trying to make a new life for myself, and I'm doing okay."

If okay involved being haunted by a ghost, but I wasn't going to trot that story out in front of just anyone. Or anyone at all, if I could help it.

8

Despite the heat of my statement, she gave me a genuine grin. "I can see that for myself, but I'm not here about your divorce settlement. Or your lack of one." I'd signed a prenuptial agreement that, according to Patrea, bordered on criminal.

"Tell me how you ended up working for Paul's family. Was it your idea, or his? Did he spend a lot of time at your office?"

Patrea's expression gave no clue to her reasons for asking, and the careful way she blanked her face as she waited for answers set my stomach to jittering. I'd been the fund-raising director for the charitable foundation run by the Hastings family until I walked out on Paul for cheating. They promptly fired me, then had security escort me out of the building.

"It was his idea. Once the excitement of the wedding and honeymoon was over, I found myself at loose ends. I left school because Paul thought we should focus on building our life together, and he thought school took up too much time."

Carried away by the romance of it all, I hadn't noticed Paul subtly exerting control over me until I walked away and took back my life.

"When he went back to work, I found myself craving something more. I'm not the type to spend my days lounging around and being pampered or whatever. So I decided to look for a job."

When Patrea made no comment, and her expression didn't change, I continued. "I kept running into walls once potential employers realized I was married to one of *those* Hastings. And finally, when Paul suggested working with the not-for-profit branch of the family business, I jumped at the chance to do something meaningful with my time. The work appealed to me. I enjoyed organizing functions, and under my direction, we raised a lot of money for various charities."

This was not news to Patrea since we'd met each other as a result of my work.

Even though we were just talking, I got the impression every word was going down on some mental notepad. "And you've had no contact with anyone from the family since you left?"

"None. I thought my sister-in-law might reach out to hear my side of the story, but it's been radio silence on all fronts."

I felt like a bug under glass when Patrea kept poking for information. "And the foundation? Any contact from there?"

9

"Nope. They cut me off like fat from a cheap steak." Losing my second family hurt, but they'd chosen to close ranks, so I was trying my best to get past the pain, and I didn't need Patrea stirring it all up again. "Why? I can't see how any of this matters now. I'm no longer part of the family. They've made that perfectly clear, and the divorce should be final in a couple of weeks."

Patrea sighed. "There's a credible rumor that the foundation is about to come under investigation for diversion of charitable funds into profit-making enterprises. Someone blew the whistle on the squeaky-clean Hastings family."

Half my body went cold, the other parts blazed hot. "That's not possible. It can't be." My fingers shook when they lifted to cover my mouth, and my mind raced through possible implications. "Was it you? Are you the whistleblower?"

You'd think I'd hit her in the forehead with a hammer by Patrea's surprised look. "No. How would I have come by that type of inside information? I figured it was you getting back at Paul for the way he treated you, so I came here to pat you on the back for being brave, and then offer my services because it was a stupid thing to do."

"Well, I didn't do anything. As the director, I was in charge of raising funds, but I had nothing to do with their disbursement. I organized events and sweet-talked donors into writing large checks. Once the money came in, the accountants took over, and my part was done."

Settling back, Patrea crossed her arms and quirked her lips into a feral smile. "The timing on this puts you in the hot seat. If there's any truth to the rumors and the news hits, you should be prepared for some blowback. It will look like you decided to do as much damage as you could on your way out of the family."

We sat in silence for a moment with Patrea watching me digest the implications and calculate the mass of the bomb she'd just dropped on me. "Or people will think I'm the one who diverted the funds. I'm the perfect scapegoat. Still, it's easy enough to prove otherwise. I wasn't authorized on any of the bank accounts, and I never signed any of the checks. My staff will vouch for me."

There was a pregnant pause from Patrea as if there was something she wanted to say and then thought better of it.

"Of anyone in the family, I had the least motive when you think about it. At least if the timing is as close as you say. The prenup put paid to me earning any benefit off the family's profits, so I'm the last person who would bother to divert funds."

When I chose to walk away without a fight over money, my decision hadn't earned me any points with Patrea. To give her credit, though, she'd been more annoyed *for* me than *at* me.

"Anyone who checks will see my bank account certainly isn't flush. I wiped out over half my money buying this house, I'm working part-time for a mortgage broker, and I drive a relic from the seventies. In my world, this is what it looks like to land on your feet, but Paul wouldn't see it that way, and neither would his family."

It seemed I'd passed some sort of test because Patrea kicked off her shoes and settled into a more comfortable position. "I'll take that coffee now. Iced if you don't mind. Then we'll lay out some contingency plans in case this debacle comes to pass." She grinned at the dismay on my face.

"Didn't I just explain my situation? You know I can't afford to hire you."

"Get me my drink, and stop worrying about the money. Some things are worth doing for their own sake, and this is one of them."

It wouldn't be polite to refuse the offer of help, or particularly bright considering my lack of other options, but because Patrea seemed a bit too invested in my welfare, I had to ask, "Did Paul or his family do something to you that I should know about?"

Feral would be the word for the smile she turned my way.

"Iced coffee." She made a scooting motion with her hand that almost annoyed me, but I stood to do her bidding anyway. "Two sugars." The order followed me out of the room while Patrea pulled a notebook from her purse and dug back in for a pen.

Halfway to the kitchen, I had an idea and came back. "Okay, but if we're doing this, you're going to come to me directly the next time you find a worthy cause, and I'll pull in a few personal favors to help you raise scads of money."

Once I had her word, I made the coffee, and when I was done, she started in with more questions.

Before she finished, she'd wrung every ounce of information she could get out of me, which wasn't as much as she'd hoped, and

11

left me feeling like a hollowed lemon half with only bits of mangled pulp clinging to my insides.

"What should I do now?"

"You should let me strip that miserable, cheating, lowlife sleazeweasel of the alimony you rightly deserve." Her face all angles and planes with bunched up features, no one would ever call Patrea a pretty woman, but when her eyes sparked with the fire of righteous anger, I saw an avenging angel. One of terrible beauty. A woman to be feared. I liked her.

"We've already had this discussion, and my stance hasn't changed, but you get points for coming up with the term sleazeweasel."

She let the topic go, made me show her the tower room, and after assuring me she'd keep in touch, Patrea offered one more piece of advice before she left.

"Don't talk to the press, and try to keep a low profile until this all blows over."

I agreed to both, but fate had other plans.

CHAPTER 2

"I'm sorry, Mrs. Lupinsky, but there's nothing I can do to help you. Once we've arranged financing, the rest is up to the mortgage provider, and they often transfer accounts between one servicing company and another."

A spate of vulgar language spewed out of my phone, and if I didn't sympathize with the woman, I might have asked Mrs. Lupinsky if she kissed her husband with that mouth. But having her mortgage transferred twice before she'd even made the first payment was a valid reason for complaint. Just not to me, because other than to make soothing noises, there wasn't a single thing I could do to help her.

"Well, Spencer could have warned me this would happen. Honestly, I could just kill him for this." The call disconnected.

I sighed and made a note to add an entry to the Frequently Asked Questions section of our paperwork and website using bold print. Mrs. Lupinsky's complaint hadn't been the first one I'd fielded during my two weeks on the job, and I didn't think it would be the last. It seemed mortgage companies traded accounts like young boys traded baseball cards. No wonder new homeowners were getting annoyed.

Being Monday, I found the company inbox stuffed full of underwriter requests, and as I relayed the last of those to the appropriate applicant, my boss appeared at my office door.

Tall and prone to arrogance, Spencer Charles looked slightly off to me as he stood framed in the opening. His tie was looser than usual and nudged a little left of center as if he'd been pulling at it because it felt tight. His hair was mussed as though he'd been running his fingers through it.

"Can you call Cassidy Chandler and tell her we're looking good to close next week?" he asked.

It sounded like a reasonable request, except that it wasn't.

"You mean lie to her?" Because over the few weeks I'd worked there, I'd developed a pretty good idea of the process, and Cassidy's complicated loan had already gone past the original closing date twice. "The sellers' agent says they won't extend again, Cassidy's a nervous wreck, and there's no way the underwriters are going to okay that deal unless she finds someone willing to cosign the loan. You're not helping her by leading her on."

"She'll have to suck it up. The agent's bluffing, the sellers will extend. I'll get the deal done, and if the underwriters don't play ball, I'll arrange for alternate financing and have her in by the end of the month at the latest. Just make the call and trust me to handle the money. I'm on top of it."

I made the call, but trusting him was a lot harder to do when he'd asked me to lie to someone whose stress level I could gauge over the phone.

Cassidy answered on the second ring. "Spencer says the sellers will extend, and he has the experience to back up the claim." I hoped. "They have your offer, and I'm sure they'd rather not have to start over. So unless someone made them a better offer, they're probably trying to provide some negative incentive for pushing the deal through."

She heaved a huge sigh. "What they're doing is making me crazy. I'm dangling over the edge here, and my fingertips are slipping. I need to know if this is going to happen or not. I have two kids sleeping in the same small room, and even with taxes and insurance, my mortgage would be lower than the rent. I need the extra money and the extra space."

I sympathized, because I knew exactly how it felt to have your life turned upside down by things over which you had no control. Not even a month earlier, I'd been a happy wife living in a nice house in the suburbs, and the director of fundraising for a multi-million dollar, non-profit organization. Now, I was well on my way to being divorced, living in a house filled with someone else's things, and to top it off, I'd been haunted by the ghost of my high school sweetheart until I'd helped him find his killer.

Okay, his killer had found me first, but it all worked out the same.

14

If it had been possible to do over the phone, I'd have given Cassidy a hug simply for the sake of solidarity.

She seemed calmer by the time we finished talking,, and I felt like a slug for giving her false hope, so I did something I hadn't done since being hired. I poked around on the office network to see if I could find her file.

Spencer had hired me to be his assistant—more of a non-job as far as I could tell. All I did was handle the correspondence between underwriters and applicants. At no point had he told me to stay out of client files, but neither had he given me permission to open them. Snooping might get me fired, but given his sketchy ethics, I wasn't sure I cared.

Except I did. Jobs were scarce in town, and I'd been turned down for enough of them that I cared plenty, but I still justified my actions. If he wasn't going to be able to help Cassidy buy a house, she deserved some advanced notice. I owed her that much, right?

Besides, if he had wanted to keep me out, he shouldn't have given me the password to access the entire network. The folder for current applications popped right up, and Cassidy's was the first one on the list. It contained all of her documentation along with a personal note from Spencer.

He had, according to the note, submitted her application to the last remaining conventional option he could try, and if refused, he would refer her loan to Quantum Funding.

Granted, I'd only been on the job for a short time, but I didn't remember getting any underwriter requests from a company by that name. Still, the time stamp on the note said it had been revised earlier in the day, so he hadn't lied when he said he was on top of things.

Feeling more optimistic on Cassidy's behalf, I forwarded all email to my phone for the rest of the day and made my way home through heat shimmering over pavement and the scent of freshly-clipped grass. Sunlight glinted off the tower windows of the old house I'd purchased for a song.

Willowby House, or Spooky Manor as I'd called it when I was younger, was not haunted—or if it was, the ghosts weren't talking to me, which amounted to the same thing—but it certainly looked the part. Gingerbread trim, a turret room, and wrought-iron fencing added to the ambiance that had every kid in town crossing Lilac street to avoid getting ghost cooties on them.

Following the loss of her beloved husband, Catherine Willowby had lived in the house alone until her health forced her into a nursing home a few weeks before her death. Since she had no other family, the house and contents eventually reverted to the town for back taxes.

I'd had the good fortune to show up on the day it went up for bids and bought the whole kit and caboodle for a shamefully small amount of money. A good investment it had turned out to be, too. Still, it was a lot of house for one person, or so everyone kept telling me.

All I wanted to do was settle in amongst Catherine's things and get my bearings.

Thankfully, she'd had excellent taste in furniture, though I considered her choice of wall coverings questionable. Every room except for the hallways boasted some variation on a fruit basket themed wallpaper. I'd had no idea there were so many options until I'd moved in.

I unlocked the door, stepped inside, and leapt half out of my skin when two things happened at the same time. A dozen cuckoo clocks went off in one of the upstairs bedrooms, and my best friend Jacy stuck her head out of the kitchen doorway.

"Good, you're home. I'm making taco soup."

"How long have you been here? Where's the Jeep?" Long enough to go upstairs and fool around with those clocks, apparently. I'd have seen Jacy's baby if it had been parked in the driveway — it was pretty hard to miss a vehicle painted bubblegum pink with a top made from striped awning material. The Jeep looked like a rolling candy store.

"Brian's dad's got it in the shop, so I walked over here after my shift. That's okay, right? I used my key. I needed the distraction today. We're supposed to get the results from the fertility clinic, and I'd rather be doing something productive than sitting home brooding and biting my nails. So, you have me for the afternoon, and you're going to put me to work."

She wagged a wooden spoon at me, and I hoped it was clean. Jacy was an excellent cook, but a messy one. "It has been weeks, and you still haven't unpacked the rest of your boxes."

16

She disappeared back into the kitchen, and I followed.

The scents of cumin and chili steaming from the pot of soup made my stomach rumble.

"I have a good feeling about the tests, and as for the unpacking, cut me a break. I'm still settling in."

"You are not. You're just rambling around in here like a guest." Droplets of soup flew as she waved the spoon at me again. "You need to make this place your own. Didn't you buy a gallon of paint to brighten up this kitchen? Or are you dragging your feet because that ass-faced pizza-freak got in here and tried to kill you? I just got my best friend back, and I don't want you to leave."

"Don't worry, I'm not going anywhere. I promise." Telling her exactly how I'd fended off my attacker wasn't in the cards. What was I supposed to say? Um, well, you see, it happened like this…Hudson's ghost shot a mannequin head down the stairs and saved my sorry butt from the pizza delivery guy who'd killed him. Yeah, that would go over like a cow in a horse race.

Jacy nodded, and some of the tension went out of her shoulders. "Good. Because I'd have to hunt you down and drag you back here if you tried to leave again."

I'd been planning on tackling the rest of my boxes anyway. "If it makes you feel better, I'll unpack today, and you can help. When we're done, we can go to the hardware store and look through wallpaper books." I directed her attention to a spot in the corner between two cabinets where I'd tested my plan to prime and paint over the worst of the wallpaper fruit-basket transgressions.

"Oh, that's not pretty."

Parts of the pattern had bled through several coats of primer and paint like a ghost that wouldn't leave.

"No, and I hate that David was right when he said that would happen."

David was the son of my father's childhood friend, and the man currently renting a room from my parents. My room, in fact. The one I'd planned to stay in when I came back home. It wasn't his fault I'd ended up staying in a motel, which led to being haunted and becoming embroiled in a murder investigation. Mostly.

And it wasn't his fault my mother had hearts in her eyes whenever she saw the two of us in a room together. David was handsome as all get out, and he'd proved to be a really nice man

17

when he'd shown up to help me on moving day. But my divorce wasn't final yet, and I wouldn't be interested in David even if it were.

Explaining this to my mother netted me her *I'm your mother, I know best* look. The one that sent my blood pressure into the red zone and caused all sorts of distance to form between us. Maybe she'd been right when she'd pegged my soon-to-be ex-husband as a playboy jerk, but that didn't make her infallible. No matter how much she pushed, I would never see David as dating material. With any luck, he'd find his own woman and move on.

Jacy dished out two bowls of soup, grated fresh cheddar over them, and tossed in some tortilla chips.

We ate for a while in comfortable silence, then she returned to the topic of the paint. "I like the color, though. That lemony yellow is so pretty against the white woodwork. Have you decided on colors for your bedroom yet?"

"No, not really. I have ideas, but then I feel weird about making changes. And don't even get me started on going through Mrs. Willowby's things," I admitted. "Isn't that silly? She's dead, so she's not going to miss any of this stuff."

Empathetic, Jacy laid a hand over mine. "I get it, sweetie."

However, along with empathy, Jacy had another special talent: that of cutting to the chase. "But you're just going to have to suck it up, dig deep, get your adult on, and take care of business." She whisked my barely emptied bowl into the dishwasher and hustled me toward the front parlor where my boxes still sat. You'd have thought it was Christmas the way she tore into them.

"Books." She pushed the first aside and pulled the tape on the second. "More books." And then a third. "Are they all books? Never mind. Where do you want them?"

Unexpectedly, the question brought tears. This was my house now, and I could put them in any room—or every room if I wanted to. I was free to choose, and it felt great. Terrifying, but mostly great. After living in Paul's house of sterile perfection, where all of my things had been declared unsuitable for public display and confined to private areas, I looked forward to living among them again.

Catherine Willowby's taste in books had run mostly to period romances, which I offered to Jacy, who was also a fan. Soon enough, we had a rhythm going. With Jacy clearing shelves ahead of me, we swapped my collection for Catherine's.

"Okay, you were right. I should have done this before because it already feels more like home."

"I am always right. You should embroider that on a pillow or something." Jacy grinned at me just as her phone rang, and when the name of the fertility clinic popped up, her face paled. Slowly, she slid her finger across the screen to answer and reached for me with her other hand.

"Hello. Yes, this is." I heard half the conversation. The hand gripping mine squeezed like a vice. "Yes. Yes, I understand. Thank you for calling."

When the call ended, Jacy froze and stared at the phone in her hand until I gave her a shake.

"What. What is it? Good news or bad?"

When she looked up, her eyes were swimming with tears, and my stomach sank.

"Oh, Jace, I'm sorry."

Then a heartbreakingly beautiful smile broke over her face. "It's good. I'm pregnant."

It didn't occur to me to feel bad that I'd found out before her husband, Brian, because the next second, we were shrieking and dancing around the living room like children. Laughing and crying at the same time. If there was a pang of envy floating around in my head, I refused to let it surface or mar the joy of the moment.

"I'm pregnant," Jacy repeated. "I can't believe this is finally happening. We've waited so long. I have to tell Brian. I have to tell my mother." Shaking hands cradled her belly. "I have to sit down. I'm giddy."

"You need to breathe. Come on now. Don't pass out on me."

"Okay." After a few seconds, she sounded calmer. For a few more seconds anyway. "I'm going to be a mother. I can do that, right? Be a mom." Then panic set in. "I'm going to be somebody's mother. How did I not realize that until right now? I mean, I wanted to have a baby, but being a mom, that's big. It's a whole other level of huge."

If she was going to freak out, it was better to get it over with now. "You can, and you're going to be so good at it. You've always been the best of us. You're a rock, and you always know the right thing to say. Plus, you had the good sense to marry a strong, decent man."

"I did." I'd always heard that pregnant women glow, but I'd never seen it happen until Jacy turned toward me, her face radiant. "You're going to have to throw me a baby shower, Auntie Everly."

"Count on it. You know I'm going to spoil the little peanut rotten."

Jacy sniffed and checked her watch. "Brian's filling in for someone in the main office, so it's hours before I can go home and tell him the good news. I need to keep busy, or I'm going to burst, so how 'bout we get the rest of these boxes unpacked? I'm going to need you all settled in and ready for babysitting duty."

More hugs followed, and more weeping, too, but high on the good news, we went back to work.

"Umm." Jacy opened one of the built-in cabinet doors. "Have you seen this? Every shelf is packed with board games. How did she get them all in here?"

I grinned. "The real question you should be asking is whether, if you take them out, you could ever get them all back in again without a diagram or something."

Sinking down to sit on the floor cross-legged, Jacy stared at the way the boxes interlocked and stacked together to fill the available space with very little room to spare. "You think she got her start in a sardine plant?"

"However it happened, she had the gift of packing. Did you see some of those games? They're really old, and I've never even heard of half of them. Uncle Wiggly, Steeplechase, Dick Tracy."

"Does she have Parcheesi? I love Parcheesi. We should do a weekly game night, and try some of these out unless you're planning to get rid of them."

Paul would have hated a weekly game night almost as much as I would love it. No, he'd hate it more. He'd have looked down on the simple pleasure of enjoying an evening laughing and competing against friends.

"I'd love that. Pick a night, and it's a date." I hunkered down next to Jacy and gave her a one-armed hug. As I did, I noticed an Ouija board among the rest of the games. "Oh, would you look at that? Do you think Mrs. Willowby had a dark side? Maybe that's where the haunted-house rumors came from."

"Maybe." It would take more than an Ouija board to impress Jacy, whose mother channeled spirit guides and filled her home with crystals. "I'm beginning to see why you've been dragging your feet. So many things in such a small space, deciding what to get rid of and what to keep. Just looking in here makes it all seem daunting."

"You ain't seen nothing yet. I'm telling you, I've opened a few of the drawers and cabinets and just closed them again because I wasn't sure where to start. I keep having visions of taking out one thing and everything else just popping out like those snakes in a can. Or worse, like clowns in a tiny car, you know?"

Jacy shuddered. "Oh, you know I hate clowns. Why did you have to put that in my head?"

"Just sharing the love."

When she reached up, I grabbed Jacy's hand and helped her up off the floor. "Looks like it's a bigger job than I thought, but that's okay." She settled on the sofa, and I took the opposite chair. "We just need a plan of attack. We'll concentrate on one room at a time, clean and clear, then move on to the next. Where do you want to start? Your bedroom? The kitchen?"

Slumping in the chair, I whined a little. "The place is growing on me. Can't I just leave it like it is?"

"And what? Become a ghost of yourself living in someone else's home?"

Ouch. The hammer went right through me as it figuratively hit the nail on the head. I sighed. "No, I suppose not." I pulled myself up to sit straight and face the task before me.

"Okay. Let's do this. We'll start... well, not in the bedroom, because that's the one room where I've made a lot of changes. Mom emptied the closet and dresser to make space for my things. I've taken over the nightstand and put out my quilts, too. Plus I rearranged the furniture, and I think I like the wallpaper. The only thing I haven't tackled is an old drop-front desk, and I'd like to put up new curtains. We should start with the room that needs the most."

Jacy brushed a lock of hair back behind her ear. "The kitchen, then?"

I considered. "No. Don't laugh, but even though there are a few things that could go, the kitchen is laid out exactly like I'd have done it myself, and I'm happy to keep clearing the clutter as I go along. Catherine had good taste in kitchenware. I just need to be brave enough to start yanking down the wallpaper."

"There you go again, making excuses and being complacent. Which room do you walk into and feel the least at home?"

"If you put it like that, it's this one." I couldn't fault Catherine's taste since each piece was of excellent quality and well-maintained, only her seeming need for quantity. "For a start, I'd get rid of everything that looks like it should be in a bedroom, then rearrange the rest of the furniture to create a better flow. Those two chairs by the door would be perfect near the fireplace."

Agreeing, Jacy added, "Then you could change out the drapes for something brighter. Maybe add a few colorful pillows, and some other accents to make everything pop."

Upholstered in a muted, peach-toned brocade, the sofa faced a pair of chairs, each flanked by small tables, and the whole works sprawled awkwardly off-center. It was an odd arrangement and obstructed the flow of the room. The rest of the furniture marched around the perimeter of the room without much thought to placement except for the most modern item, a combination rocking chair and recliner in the prime television-watching spot.

"While this room is easily the largest, I think she did most of her entertaining in that front room. Mrs. Dexter over at the Bide A Way mentioned Catherine used to throw parties at Halloween. I bet we'll find a slew of decorations tucked away somewhere."

While the sun moved from one end of the house toward the other, we shifted two dressers into the bedroom to be emptied later, relegated several extra end tables and a console table to the garage, and moved the pretty, glass-doored shelf to a better spot.

"You were right to force me into this," I admitted to Jacy as we grunted and tugged the heavy sofa into place. "Faced this way and with the chairs angled on either side, the whole room opens up and becomes more inviting. Plus, now there's room for those two smaller chairs in front of the fireplace like I pictured them." I had visions of reading a good book and toasting my toes near the flames while a storm raged outside.

Sweat beading over her triumphant grin, Jacy said, "I am always right. It's my superpower."

Cocking an eyebrow, I pointed out that I had photographic proof of some of her fashion fails, and we laughed over old times while we oozed sweat and hauled the rest of the furniture into position.

Because it was a day of good news and embracing the future, I didn't tell her about Patrea's visit or the new worry looming on my horizon.

"Have you picked out baby names yet?"

Barking out a short laugh, Jacy fluttered a hand at me. "Don't even get me started. Did you know Brian's grandfather's name was Dignity? Dignity. That's what he wants to name our son if we have a boy. And I'm not saying there's anything wrong with an unusual name, but if I name my kid Dignity Dean, he's gonna get teased at school."

"Probably so." I tried to stifle a smile. "What about if it's a girl?"

"Oh, that's even worse. My mother and Brian are in cahoots with the *its a word, but we can use it as a name* thing. She's pushing for Calm if it's a girl."

I couldn't stop the snort.

"Don't you laugh, it gets worse." Now Jacy was giggling. "Brian suggested Morning, so now they've landed on a compromise. Calm Morning. It sounds more like a weather report than a name. Couldn't you just die?"

"Well, you have to admit, it's unique." I kind of liked it, but I could see Jacy didn't want to hear that opinion.

"Hah, a lot you know. Unique was on the list, too. Along with Virtue and Rain. If I don't put my foot down, my kid will end up being called Cornflake or Basket or something worse. When Momma Wade and Brian get on the same page, it's hard to close the book. You'll back me up, right? I mean, you're going to be my second coach in the delivery room, so you'll be right there to put a stop to any weird name shenanigans, won't you?"

How could I say no? "I will. I've got your back." And that was where I planned to stay during the delivery.

"Okay, that's settled, then." Visibly relieved, Jacy stuck her hands on her hips and surveyed the room. "Looks better, don't you think?"

The new arrangement suited me fine. "My shins thank you for the bruises they will no longer be forced to bear from those end tables."

"Good. Now, we'll hit the hardware store, and then you can pay me back by dropping me off so I can pick up my Jeep. I need to hit the grocery store for steaks and a bottle of their best sparkling cider to celebrate. If I can't have champagne, Brian can suffer along with me."

CHAPTER 3

When the kitchen timer buzzed to let me know I needed to marinate the chicken, I was hunkered down with a bobby pin trying to pick a door lock. Nearly a month after moving in, the key to the newest part of the house still hadn't turned up anywhere, and the suspense was getting to me.

Not enough to bust the door down, or to pay for a locksmith since there were plenty of other rooms that needed attention. Enough to test my skills with every video guide to lock-picking I could find, though. Maybe it was me, maybe it was the videos, but so far, nothing I'd tried had worked.

I was just tucking the second sprig of rosemary in with the chicken when the doorbell chimed.

"You're early," I yelled down the hall. More than three hours early, and there went my chance to shower and change my clothes before my parents showed up for dinner. I hadn't planned to greet them still covered in a sheen of sweat from hauling the dust covers off the last of the furniture in the upstairs rooms.

Internally griping, I didn't pay much attention to who was on the other side of the textured glass when I yanked open the door.

A whirl of brown fur shot past me with a scrabbling of toenails on the floor and arrowed straight into the kitchen, leaving the ripe scent of damp dog behind. Torn between looking for the owner and making sure my chicken was still safe, I cast a hasty glance down both sides of the street, I left the door open and chose my chicken.

The dog, a mud-covered chocolate lab, rose up on its hind legs and took a swipe at the refrigerator door handle, clearing off at least half a dozen of Mrs. Willowby's collection of magnets. The dog had probably used the same technique to ring my doorbell. I moved the chicken out of reach and went back to the porch to scan the street for a possible owner.

Seeing none, I went back into the kitchen just in time to see him or her take another swipe at the handle. When mournful brown eyes turned my way, I caved.

"Are you hungry?"

Yeah, I knew it was a stupid question, but that didn't stop me asking it, and I got my answer when the dog frantically wiggled and danced in circles.

"Okay. Let's see what we can find."

I dug through the leftovers, came up with a container of chicken and rice that I thought wouldn't be too spicy for a dog's digestion, and offered it to my uninvited guest. Taking a chair, I waited while the dog slurped up the contents at something like twice the speed of light, then treated me to an indelicate belch.

She, or at least I assumed it was a she now that she wasn't in motion and I could see a hot pink collar peeking through the brown, showed her gratitude by placing her head on my knee.

"You are a pretty one, aren't you?"

Under the damp mud clinging to her sides, her fur looked smooth, and her eyes were clear and friendly. A length of leash trailed behind her, the end ragged and torn, and when I gently petted her head, she gazed up at me with adoration.

"Let's see who you belong to, okay? I'm just going to look at your tags."

Her head was almost as big as mine, so I moved carefully. There was no aggression in her, though. Her tongue gently swiped across my hand as I reached for her collar and turned it so I could read the personalized buckle.

Her name was Molly, and she belonged to my boss, Spencer Charles. Coincidence? Not in my weird little world.

"Well, Molly"—she shimmied in ecstasy when she heard her name—"Let's see if we can get you back to where you belong. Your owner has some explaining to do."

Technically, I wasn't the one who deserved to hear why Spencer had missed another closing on Friday that would have to be rescheduled—that honor went to the family who wouldn't be waking up in their new house tomorrow. But I did want to know why he'd gone MIA and still wasn't answering his phone.

I sacrificed a towel to the cause of getting the big dog presentable enough to be allowed in my car and drove old Sally

Forth—the name I'd given the '79 Buick I'd unwittingly purchased along with the house—out to the address listed on her collar. Spencer lived in the only section of what could loosely be called tract housing in town.

A three-acre plot carved out of what had once been a potato field held a pair of vertical-sided, stone-faced, modern homes with vast expanses of slanted roof that looked out of place in a modest, northeastern town. Exactly, I thought as soon as I laid eyes on the place, where I would have pictured Spencer living if I'd ever taken the notion to think about it.

For the quarter-mile before we turned down his road, Molly had been alternately whining and making the doggy equivalent of a grumbling noise—half growl, half short bark. Her agitation unsettled me.

While the two houses on the lot were mirror images of each other, the resemblance ended at the design of the structures themselves. The one Spencer lived in, according to the number on Molly's collar, lacked a single detail to make it look like a home.

In contrast, the second yard bloomed with flowering shrubs behind a lovely rustic fence. A swing set and a trampoline took up one side of the lawn, a small garden plot the other.

Molly seemed more interested in staring back the way we had come than in being home, and when I opened the back door, she made a run for the end of the driveway before I had a chance to grab the trailing end of her leash.

When I tried to follow on foot, she took off down the road, leaving me no choice but to get back in the car and drive after her. At the spot where she'd begun whining, she looked back at me, banked left, and trotted down the entrance road to the town transfer station and recycling center.

I slowed to a stop, and she ran back toward me, barked twice, and then headed back the way she had come. The hint wasn't especially subtle—she wanted me to follow her, and so I did. Right up to the locked gate. Being the third Saturday of the month, the landfill was closed, and wouldn't open until the next day to give those who only had Sundays free a chance to drop off their trash.

Eerily silent other than the occasional yips from Molly, the place was utterly deserted, which, I figured, was the reason for the

27

sudden sense of dread clawing at my throat. But I pushed open the fence and followed the dog toward the three-sided recycling shed.

Only half of the roll-down metal grates were closed, which wasn't normal since the center should have been locked up tight.

Head down now, Molly slowed her pace as she passed through the opening, skirted a bucket loader, and made for the rear of the building. I was still ten feet behind her when she reached the ledge overlooking a six-foot dropped-down section where the industrial paper shredder emptied out. Someone must have run it recently because the pile of paper rose high over the top of the abutment.

Leg muscles bunching, the dog readied herself for the leap down.

I shouted, "Molly! Stop!" But I was too late. At least she landed on the pile of paper and not unforgiving concrete. Ignoring the posted warnings, I stepped into the danger zone designated by orange stripes painted on the concrete and looked down.

My instincts shrieked something was wrong. Very, very wrong.

Molly pawed at the ribbons of paper, then sat on her haunches and let out an unearthly, keening howl. I didn't want to go closer, but I searched for a way down and found a set of stairs partially hidden behind the controls shed to my left. As I came closer, Molly whined and began to dig in earnest.

Paper flew. I reached down to help and saw the hand sticking out from under the pile.

It was too late. I knew that before I steeled myself to check the wrist for a pulse, and my fingers touched chilled skin.

My hands shook when I tapped out 9-1-1 to report the body and didn't stop even after Ernie Polk's black-and-white pulled up behind old Sally.

"Everly."

"Ernie."

"You planning on making a habit out of finding dead bodies?"

A bubble of hysterical laughter gurgled in the back of my throat, but I bit it back and willed myself to breathe until it passed.

"I sincerely hope not. I'm pretty sure it's Spencer Charles."

The passing thought that Ernie's eyebrows looked like caterpillars when they shot up under the salt-and-pepper hair that rode low on his forehead proved my hysteria wasn't fully under control.

"What now? You're carrying an ID kit in your purse these days?"

"No." I shoved my hands in my pockets because my fingertips had begun to feel numb. "But I recognize his watch, and that's his dog." I nodded my head toward Molly, who had stationed herself nearby as though standing watch over her master. "She brought me here."

How she'd managed to show up at my house was a mystery I didn't plan on laying out for Ernie's speculating pleasure since I hadn't had time to cook up a believable explanation. If there was one to be had at all, which probably wasn't the case.

"He's my boss, and he hasn't been answering calls or emails since yesterday, so I came over to see if anything was wrong. Molly must have been with him when it happened because she led me here."

My answer didn't seem to mollify Ernie.

"You're on a first-name basis with your boss's dog?"

The fire of annoyance burned off the last of my nerves. "Her name and his address are on her collar. I didn't have anything to do with the man outside of work, and frankly, didn't have a whole lot of contact with him on the job, either."

With Spencer presumably dead—we wouldn't know for sure until the body was exhumed from the pile of paper—I was, once again, out of a job. Apparently losing jobs and finding dead people was my new normal.

After calling in for assistance, Ernie followed me to the body. He checked for signs of life, and finding none, ran me through my story two more times.

"Yes, the doors were open when I got here. I haven't touched a thing except for his hand to see if he had a pulse." Other than glossing over the dog's appearance on my doorstep, I told him the full truth.

Molly sidled up to me and leaned in hard against my leg. Absently, I rubbed her ears and said to Ernie, "Do I need to tell you where I was at the time of the murder?"

Sirens wailed in the distance.

"Unless you know something I don't," Ernie folded his arms over his chest, "this looks like an unfortunate accident to me. I happen to know a little bit about how the shredder works. The system was designed for safety. Whole thing runs off a set of timers controlled by a computer program, so it's mostly automated. It's even got scanners to make sure nothing but paper goes through the knives."

"If it's so safe, how can you call this an accident?"

Ernie huffed once, then took my arm and pointed up. "That's the chute, see? Paper comes in by the bag or bin and gets dumped into the shredding hopper that feeds into the building over there." His pointing finger moved left.

"The hopper holds half a ton of paper. When it's full, the operator—that's my brother-in-law, by the way—starts the program. From then, everything runs off a set of timers. Hydraulic doors seal off the input end of the machine, and everything goes on lockdown while the paper feeds through the shredder."

Since it didn't look like Spencer had been shredded, I couldn't see how Ernie arrived at his theory of accidental death, but I let him talk.

"The entire load of processed paper dumps out of the shredder and down into that chute. The doors won't even open until the cutters wind down. During business hours when there are people in the building, there's an override to open the doors manually, but it's set to auto when there's no one around. Paper collecting services have a key to the hopper, so they can dump even on closed days. There's a weight-operated switch in the bottom of the hopper that kicks the system on once the load limit's reached. I figure that's what happened."

Sometime during the long-winded explanation, my brain glazed over because I still didn't understand, and I told him so.

"Looks to me like someone made an early delivery of enough paper to trigger the system to run through the shredding cycle. Spencer had the bad luck to be standing here when it dumped."

"Sounds reasonable, but you said the system was built for safety. Wouldn't there be an alarm of some kind? For that matter, couldn't someone have lured him down there and then triggered the chute doors manually?"

Ernie looked at me with a flat stare. "Do you want it to be murder?"

"No, of course, I don't. It's just hard to understand how something like this could happen. How did he get in? And why would he go down there?"

If for no other reason than to mollify me, Ernie mounted the stairs, pulled down the metal gate, and inspected the latch. I followed just in time to see him let go of the door and watch it rise on its own.

"See, the latch is busted, and the tension on the roller is too tight, so the door goes up by itself. No great mystery."

"That still doesn't explain what he was doing down there in the danger zone," I insisted.

Heaving a sigh, Ernie roamed the area near the pile of paper and looked for clues. I heard him sigh two more times before he came back into sight. "Paper's buried anything that might give me a clue. You can trust that I'll do my best to figure out what happened, but it's pretty obvious he was in the wrong place at the wrong time. Helluva way to go."

My imagination supplied a shudder-worthy reenactment of Spencer's death. "Will you let me know if you find anything?"

"I will, but I checked, and the control room is still locked, so there's no way anyone could have triggered the doors. Had to be an accident. Could be the alarm didn't sound and he never saw it coming."

My eyes trailed back to the hand sticking out from beneath the pile of paper. "I hope you're right." I didn't see how it could have happened any other way. "What will you do with Molly?"

"I'll call the dog catcher, and I suppose she'll go to the pound until someone from his family steps forward."

Ernie had hunkered down to take photos of the hand from various angles. Once he was finished, he carefully moved enough paper to uncover the dead man's face.

After a quick glance, I looked away and heard Ernie's gust of a sigh, then the whir of his phone camera as he took a picture.

"What if no one in his family wants her?"

He shrugged, shot a couple more close-ups, then pulled out his phone to make the call.

I didn't even have to think twice.

31

"Wait. Do you have to do that? Or is it okay if I take her? She's a sweet dog, and if someone from the family steps forward, at least she won't have had to go to the pound in the meantime."

"Fine by me, and you're free to go. I'll stop by if I have any more questions."

Again, I didn't think twice. I didn't want to be there when they pulled Spencer's body out.

A mortgage broker buried under a mountain of paperwork. There was a certain sense of poetic justice to the death that was hard to ignore.

CHAPTER 4

About halfway home, I had indulged in a few sniffles over the trauma of finding a body, and the loss of a man I barely knew, but mostly for poor Molly, when she let out a short bark and went berserk in the back seat. Old Sally swerved a little when I jumped at the sound, and then a lot when Spencer materialized in my passenger seat.

I said something to the effect of *oh no, not again*, though with a few swear words tossed in, then pulled over to the side of the road before I crashed the car.

"No. Nope. No," I exclaimed, shaking my head. "I am not doing this. You go along now, and look for the light." I made a little shooing motion toward him.

In what I could only assume was delight, Molly tried to spin in circles on the back seat. Mostly, she managed to whip the back of my head with her tail a few times before Spencer was able to calm her down.

Finally, she settled and rested her chin next to the headrest on the back of his seat.

"There's my good girl." She didn't even flinch when he ran a ghostly hand through her head, but I knew from experience, touching a ghost brought on an unnerving chill. "Thanks for taking her. You won't be sorry. She's great company."

Right. Because talking about his dog was the most important topic to discuss.

"It's my pleasure, but enough about Molly. Can you tell me anything about how you ended up dead?" History suggested he couldn't, but I didn't think it would hurt to ask since I only had the one past experience to work from.

Since I'd twisted around in the seat to get a better look at him, I saw the way his form wavered while he tried to formulate an answer.

The air in the car seemed to vibrate with the force of his attempt and set a tingle in the back of my throat that bordered on painful.

"I want to, but I can't."

Goosebumps rose on my skin as air already cooled from having the A/C running chilled enough to form frost on the inside of my windows.

"Okay, calm down. You're freaking me out here. Ernie says it was an accident."

He wouldn't be here if it were, but a girl can hope.

"How stupid are you? Someone killed me, and since you're my assistant, you're going to help me find out who."

He wasn't any nicer as a ghost than he'd been as a man. "Why are you such a jerk? How can you have worked in a service-related industry and not realize people respond better when you treat them with dignity?"

Yeah, sitting in my car, lecturing the ghost of my former boss was just how I wanted to spend my day.

"You're going to help me because that's the kind of person you are, so how about you just get on with it?"

"Look, I have company coming for dinner, and I need to go home and get Molly settled. Why don't you just go look for the light, and let me be? We're not friends, and you're not my boss any more."

I might have been able to ignore his plaintive look, but I couldn't resist the way Molly responded to it. With a soft, whining sigh, she tilted her head and looked at me. I caved.

"Fine. You're right. I'll do what I can to help you, but there are rules." This was not my first time, and he didn't need to know there wasn't a thing I could do to stop him from haunting me.

"First rule, don't expect me to talk to you when there are other people around. Second rule, respect my personal space. You don't show up in my bedroom, or my bathroom. Ever. Third rule, don't ask me to give your family any goodbye messages from beyond the grave."

34

The inside of the car had just warmed up enough for my goosebumps to settle, but they prickled and flared again. "That's really cold," Spencer said.

"Oh, you're one to talk. Cut the theatrics." The air came back up a few degrees.

"You won't have to pass on any messages. My parents are gone, and my sister hasn't spoken to me since Mom's funeral. Molly was my family."

Well, that was sad, but I didn't want to hear the story right then. Finding his body had put me right on the edge of my emotional limit for the day, and I needed to go home and finish getting dinner ready. Not only because I had company coming, but also to give my emotions time to settle.

"My folks are coming to dinner. I can't put them off." I needed the comfort of them. "Which means you're going to stay away until they're gone. Then we'll talk, and I'll see if I can figure out what happened to you."

I softened a little when I saw him looking at Molly with regret. "I promise I'll give Molly a good home, and maybe when her time on earth is over, she'll find you in whatever place it is you go when you go into the light."

His *thank you* seemed heartfelt, and he obliged by fading away.

My fingers barely shook when I put the car in gear and pulled back out onto the road. I took that as a sign of progress. We will not talk about the absurdity of considering the ability to shake off a case of the heebie-jeebies as a personal accomplishment.

On the plus side, being haunted again drove Paul and the worry about his dastardly deeds right out of my head. Maybe calling that a positive was pushing things a little, but a girl's gotta do what she's gotta do to get by.

The bad news had beaten me back to the grocery store even though Carol Ann Wilmette hadn't been on dispatch, and I wondered if I'd been wrong about her being ground zero for rumor central. People had just stopped looking at me funny from the last murder, and I didn't even make it to the dog food aisle before I realized my reprieve had ended.

Two men loosely tied to me and found dead within weeks of my moving back to town was too much of a coincidence. People I'd

35

known my entire life pushed their grocery carts a little faster to get out of my way. It hurt, but mostly it ticked me off, so I sailed through the store, picked out a huge bag of dog food for Molly, and smiled at everyone I saw along the way. No use in making a scene.

Until I stepped up behind my co-worker, Robin, at the checkout, and she turned toward me. Blotchy red patches covered her face, and her eyelids were puffy. I wasn't sure what to say to her, and as it turned out, I didn't have to decide.

As soon as Robin laid eyes on me, she let out a wail and launched herself into my arms, knocking the bag of dog food to the floor in the process. So much for keeping a low profile.

I patted her on the back, said a few words of consolation, and eventually got us both through the line.

"What am I going to do without him?"

It had already hit me that I'd just become jobless again, and so had Robin, but that wasn't what she meant, because when I said we'd find other work somehow, she launched into another bout of sobbing.

"Don't you see? My life is over. He was my all, my everything. My one true love."

As I helped her load groceries into her car, she continued on in that vein, and I couldn't figure how I'd missed the signs of a torrid office romance going on right under my nose. Spencer hadn't paid any more attention to her than a man would pay any employee, and he'd even said some things that came off as slightly disparaging. But then again, I hadn't been too impressed with his manners, so that might have just been his way, and plenty of women end up with men who have jerk tendencies.

When she started fishing for particulars on how he'd died, I said, "I'm sorry. I have to go. You see, I have Mo—"

"Don't tell her about the dog or she'll fight you for custody." Spencer popped up to my right, and I jumped about a mile. "Please. Molly hates Robin."

I was not about to get into a dog custody fight with Robin in the middle of a public space, so I changed the end of the sentence to *my parents coming for dinner* and made my getaway with Spencer following behind.

"You shouldn't date people your dog doesn't like," I said in a low tone. "You know they're good judges of character."

"I wasn't dating Robin."

"She doesn't seem to know that."

"I was only sleeping with her."

"Oh."

Leaving me to consider that piece of *too much information*, Spencer evaporated, and I tried to put a lock on seeing any unwanted mental images as I drove home.

Molly dodged my attempt at snapping on the new leash I'd bought and nearly dumped me in the driveway in her haste to find an appropriate spot in the backyard to do her business.

"Not there," I yelled, too late to save her flattening a cluster of lilies. "Oh, Molly."

"Don't yell at her." Spencer popped up again. "She's still a puppy."

"I didn't yell at her, did I? I yelled to her, there's a difference." Then the rest of his sentence registered. "She's still a puppy?" Good grief. She stood taller than my waist already. "How old is she? Is she still growing?"

"About nine months, and no, I don't think she'll get any bigger than she is now. She's just suffering from spatial dissonance." When I stared, he elaborated. "She doesn't realize she's as big as she is. When her brain catches up to her body, she'll calm down a lot. In the meantime, she needs plenty of love and understanding."

Two words I wouldn't have pegged him for having in his repertoire, much less his vocabulary.

"Okay, why don't you run along to wherever it is ghosts go when they're not pestering the living. I'm not going to yell at the dog." I sighed as I watched her make the return trip through the patch of lilies. "She'll need to learn some manners, though. Won't you, girlie girl?"

Molly had returned to my side and plastered herself against my leg. "Come inside, and we'll get you settled. I'll take good care of her, I promise. And remember, if you want my help, you'll stay away while my parents are visiting." My caution fell on empty air—he'd already gone.

Grumbling to myself, I shifted the bag of dog food into my left arm, unlocked the door, and then stumbled when Molly shoved past me to get inside. Her tail whipping in circles, the dog checked out

37

every open room and finally returned to sprawl across a patch of sun near the table.

She snored gently as I fired up the oven and slid the pan of chicken in to bake. My folks were due in an hour, so I left her there to sleep and headed for the bathroom to get cleaned up and ready for company.

CHAPTER 5

Help me.

Seeing those two words scrawled on my bathroom mirror sent my pulse racing, but not out of fear.

"Spencer! Can you hear me? I meant what I said. The bathroom is off-limits." I didn't expect to get a response, and I wasn't disappointed. "And really? Could you have chosen anything more cliché?"

Again, no response. "Stay away until my parents leave, or our deal is off," I reminded what was probably thin air, and tucked the towel more tightly around me.

The delay of checking my bedroom for pockets of cold air before getting dressed put me a little behind, so when the doorbell rang, I ran fingers through my hair and left it to dry naturally.

Molly beat me to the door, but only because she body-checked me on her way past, doing the doggy dance of pleasure.

"Everly! Is everything okay in there?" I heard my dad's voice and saw his figure through the textured glass before the knob turned. The door swung wide just as I lunged for Molly's collar and missed.

"No!" I was too late. Muscles bunched, shining fur rippled, and the rest happened in a blur that ended with my father pinned against the wall while Molly kissed every inch of his face.

"I, uh, got a dog." I offered, though at that point I was stating the obvious.

"So I see. And what is his name?" I couldn't tell by the look on my mother's face whether she approved or not.

"Her. Her name is Molly." I made to grab her collar, and this time, I didn't intend to miss.

"Molly! Down!" I'd heard my mother use that voice a time or two during my upbringing, but I'd had no idea it worked on dogs. You learn something new every day.

Capitulating to the voice of authority, Molly dropped and showed off her best doggy grin. Once again, I had to give the dog credit for knowing her audience when Dad handed me the wine bottle he carried and started talking baby talk to her.

Mom gave me a half-smile. "We'll leave these two to get acquainted, and you can tell me why you decided to get a dog while you show me what you've done with the kitchen." I still couldn't tell what she was thinking, so I led the way.

"Why, it doesn't look like you've changed a thing." Again with the neutral tone.

To hide my thoughts, I went to the stove and took a peek at the chicken. "I suppose you're right. Can I assume you haven't heard the bad news?"

"I guess not. We took a lovely ride around the lake and came straight here."

"There's been—"

My doorbell rang a split second before the front door opened and slammed my dad, who was still sitting in the hallway talking earnestly to Molly, in the leg.

"Ow!" He yelped and pulled his leg back to let in a wide-eyed Jacy.

"Sorry, Mr. D. I didn't mean to bump into you like that. Where's Everly?" Without leaving time for an answer, I heard Jacy yell. "Everly, where are you?"

"In the kitchen."

She blew into the kitchen like a whirlwind."Hey, whose dog? There you are. I came as soon as I heard. Are you okay? I can't believe this is happening again."

Perplexed, my mother cut through the spate of questions because she knew that once Jacy got on a roll, there wasn't any other option. "What's happened?"

"As I was about to tell you, Spencer Charles died this morning, or maybe last night."

"Rumors are flying all over town, so I had to come find out for myself," Jacy turned worried eyes my way. "Did you really find his body in the recycling center? People are saying he left you a

40

voicemail right before he went through the shredder, and the only thing left of him was a hand." She shuddered, and my mother's face went a pale, probably from the mental image Jacy conjured.

"No, he didn't go through the shredder, but yes, I did find his body."

Jacy flung her hands in the air. "That's it. You'll be asking me to help pack your things by the end of the week, and who could blame you? You haven't even been back for two months, and look at the run of bad luck you've had."

"Seems to me that Spencer's luck was worse. If you want to know what really happened, you'll stop planning my life and listen for a minute."

I gave them the abridged version from the time Molly showed up on my doorstep to my asking Ernie for permission to take Spencer's dog home with me. I only left out the part where he came along for the ride.

Halfway through, I had to get up and turn the oven off to keep the chicken from drying out, and when I settled back at the table, my mother said, "You seem fairly calm, all things considered."

What was I supposed to say to that? *He's still hanging around, leaving notes on my mirror, and invading my privacy, so he doesn't feel dead to me.* Yeah, sure. That would go over well.

"I'm not sure it's hit me yet," seemed the safest answer. "Now, can we move on to something more suited to polite conversation around the dinner table? Jace, you're welcome to stay for what I can only assume by now is dried out lemon chicken."

Wisely, she declined, and once we were all settled in to eat, I dropped the second bombshell of the day.

"I had a visit from that attorney I spoke to after Paul and I split. She came to warn me that there might be trouble with the foundation." While I outlined the situation, I could see my mother gearing up for an I told you so.

Dad viciously stabbed his fork into a second piece of chicken that had surprisingly not been too dry to eat. "This attorney, is she any good?"

"She is."

"I hear a but." My mother picked up on my reservations.

"But, I think she has some sort of history with the family, and I don't want to end up in the middle of a vendetta without knowing

41

all the facts. I've asked why she's so dead set that they're bad people, but she keeps dodging the question."

My mother siding with Patrea was a given since they agreed when it came to my ex-husband and his family. My father's outburst came across as something of a surprise.

"Good!" he all but bellowed. "She'll work all the harder if she has a personal stake in the outcome. Do you need money for a retainer? I could cash in my 401K."

Touched by the offer, I quickly assured him I had it covered, and then watched him spear a third piece of chicken. Suspicious, I leaned over and looked under the table.

"I guess Molly's already had her evening meal. How much did you give her?"

"Just the one piece," he said without looking me in the eye.

"So two?"

My mother gave him the raised eyebrow treatment, and he caved. "Yeah. She looked at me with those eyes, and I couldn't help myself."

Rising, my mother circled the table, got Molly's attention, and ordered her from the room in the same firm tone she'd used earlier.

That done, she returned to her seat and said to me, "As a first-time dog owner, I think you and Molly might both benefit from a training and discipline class. Just to learn the ropes. I know someone local if you're interested. Her name is Christine Murray. Would you like her number?"

"Please. Or maybe you can teach me how to use the mom voice on her. That seems to work."

I saw a flicker of something that looked a bit like regret pass over her face, but she didn't bring up the subject of grandchildren, so I considered that conversational ball dodged. "So this Christine, is she another new transplant to town?"

"No, her maiden name is Polk. You'd have gone to school with her, though she'd have been a few years ahead of you."

Christine Polk, as I dredged a face up from memory, hadn't run in the same circles as my friends and me. A tall, rawboned girl who wore jeans and flannel and muck boots to school, she hadn't fit in with the more outgoing crowd.

"I remember her." Vaguely, anyhow. She was Ernie's younger sister, so she would also be the wife of the guy in charge of the

42

shredder at the recycling center. All the more reason to sign up for a class. "Give me her number, and I'll call tomorrow."

An hour later, I'd just cleaned up after dinner and settled in my new favorite spot on the sofa in the living room, a book in hand, when Spencer decided to pop back in and scare the bejesus out of me. I shivered and pulled the crocheted throw blanket from the back of the couch down around my shoulders.

"You have to learn to give me some kind of warning when you're going to do that," I griped, knowing it was a losing battle. What exactly could I do to an incorporeal form? Absolutely nothing, that's what, but it wasn't going to stop me from complaining whenever he showed up unannounced.

He glared at me for a moment and snapped, "You know, this is new for me, too. It's not like I've ever been dead before. If you want me gone, help me, and then I'll go."

"I *said* I'd help you, but you're going to have to give a little, buddy. If you can't tell me about your death, how about you tell me about your life? Leave out the part where you learned all your people skills from a troll. On second thought, maybe that's the part you need to focus on since that's probably what got you killed."

Yeah, maybe I was unnecessarily harsh, and I realized it as soon as I saw Spencer's face fall. "Point taken," was his reply, and that made it even worse.

"Look, I'm sorry, really," I apologized, and I meant it. " I'm not exactly used to this either. Let's just try to figure this out as fast as possible so we can both be free."

"What do you want to know?" Spencer said after several long seconds of deliberation. As if he had any more choice than I did.

"Well, for one thing, did you have any enemies?" It seemed like a moot question since he obviously had at least one person out for his blood, but I asked it anyway.

Spencer shook his head, "no, nobody specific that I can think of. At least, nobody with enough of a grudge to resort to murder."

"How about friends, then? Who did you spend your time with, aside from Robin?" My wayward brain tried to supply a mental image of them doing it, and I wished I hadn't brought her up.

I also earned myself another cold, ghostly glare, and shivered again. "I had a group of guy friends who would get together for poker, but otherwise, I tended to keep to myself. Molly here was enough companionship after spending all day dealing with people."

"Okay," I said, my heart wrenching a little at the look he shot his—now my—dog. "Give me their names, and I'll go from there." I scribbled the list on a pad of paper. "What about your family? You said something about your sister being mad at you. Exactly how mad was she?"

Spencer began to pace around the room, or as close to a pace as a ghost can get. It was more like a glide, and his edges blurred a little as he moved. I'd never seen him, while he was still living, allow himself to get so flustered.

"It wasn't like that. We haven't spoken to each other for over two years. We didn't get along all that well before, but it was just kid stuff. Then, when our mother died about a year after Pop went, we had a major fight. She called me an insensitive ingrate, and I suppose she was right. I've never been good at people and relationships. Neither has she."

He was being cagey, and it irked, but I'd learned my lesson about acting snarky and decided to take a different approach.

"I'm sure that was a tough situation," I said. "And your sister probably didn't kill you, but it might make a difference if I had more details. What were your parents like?"

"Fine, if you must know. My father was a hard man. Critical of everything, yelled at everyone if they didn't do things exactly the way he wanted. He was hard to live with because he only acted that way with family. Sometimes, I act just like him."

Spencer's story only made me more thankful for my family. My mom and I might butt heads on occasion, but I'd never, not for a minute, doubted her love for me.

"Anyway, when my mother passed, Kendra was too distraught to handle any of the details. I was the executor of the will, and when I tried to wrap up probate quickly and efficiently, she didn't want to hear anything about it. It wasn't like either of us was going to live in the house, and I thought it would be best to sell quickly. Kendra thought I was out for the money, ripped me a new one, and told me to go … pleasure myself in a way that wasn't physically possible. We got into it, and I said some things, she said I was dead to her, and I guess she meant it because we haven't spoken since."

He hadn't given me any leads, but I did gain some insight into Spencer's character, which might help me find his killer.

CHAPTER 6

The sun was up, but I wasn't when a motor sputtered to life outside my bedroom window and sent Molly into a full-on, doggy-style freakout. Without warning, she landed in the middle of the bed like she'd been dropped there from the ceiling, and barked at the window like a maniac.

Gathering up what breath she hadn't knocked out of me, I begged her to be quiet and tried to shove her off my chest. Not the easiest thing to do from a prone position. We struggled for a minute or so until I persuaded her to get down. The second her weight came off me, I hauled myself out of bed and twitched aside the curtains to see David sweep past the window on the old riding lawn mower that had been in my garage when I moved in.

As much as I appreciated his determination to be helpful, he seemed to be suffering from a complete lack of boundaries. I'd locked the garage behind me the day before, which meant my dad must have revealed the location of my hide-a-key.

In a double rush because Molly had begun pacing between me and the door, I tossed on whatever clothes came to hand and clipped on her new leash.

"Okay, girl. Just hang on a minute and let me get the door open." If she hadn't reached her full growth, I really wasn't sure I'd be able to handle her when she did. That fact was borne out when the door finally opened, and she lunged down the steps with her eyes pinned on her favorite peeing spot.

The mower rounded the corner as Molly dragged me down the steps, and I heard the dying whine of the whirling blade as David twisted the switch and cut off the engine.

A smile on his face, he dismounted and approached. "Hey, you got a dog."

It was barely eight am, I hadn't had my coffee, the dog had trampled on my bladder, the gate was open, so I wasn't sure if I should let her out alone, and she wasn't the only one who had to pee. For all those reasons, I snapped at David and then felt bad for doing it.

"Sorry. I'm just … would you mind?" I handed him the leash. "I'll be right back."

I heard him talking to Molly as I raced back inside and took care of my own morning business. When I stepped back outside afterward, David was down on one knee talking to Molly, who regarded him with a tilted head and solemn expression.

I'd have liked to have heard whatever he said to her, but I wasn't about to ask. "If you want me to put more than two coherent words together, I'm going to need coffee. Want a cup?" Anything to get him off the loud mower until my brain kicked into gear.

Reaching out, David handed back the leash. "Sure. Nice dog, by the way. What's her name?"

"This is Molly. She belonged to Spencer Charles. You heard about him, I assume."

News travels fast in small towns. He'd heard.

"They were going to send Molly to the pound, so I volunteered to take her instead. I think she's going to be good company for me once she settles in a bit. She's very sweet even if she's not altogether graceful at times."

Being in a new house was something I understood well enough. Like Molly, some of my first few nights here had been restless ones where I'd come awake at every new sound, and the house made plenty of them. Creaks and groans and weird settling noises that might have been creepy if the place really was haunted. In a grand twist of fate, Spooky Manor had been completely ghost-free until I moved in and brought one with me.

"Chocolate labs need a lot of exercise and a firm hand." As a simple statement of fact, what he said sounded perfectly reasonable. His tone carried all sorts of context, the gist of which I took to mean he didn't think I was up to the job.

I'd forgiven David for taking over my childhood room even if I still hadn't heard the reason why he was staying with my folks. I'd admitted, even in front of Jacy, that he was a nice guy, but why did he feel the need to turn every conversation into a lecture?

47

So I snapped at him. "I know that." Hadn't I made her sleep on a pile of folded blankets on the floor instead of joining me on the bed? "I'm signing us up for a training class later on today. I have it covered."

He raised a brow at my tone. The man might be attractive, but I found David annoying on several other levels—and not the kind of annoying that carried latent sparks of romance, despite what my mother thought. I might not have any firsthand knowledge about sibling rivalry, but I'd spent enough time with Jacy's family to recognize the signs.

"Sorry. I'm not at my best today." He'd followed me inside and looked out of place leaning against the counter while I filled the coffee maker and poured kibble into Molly's bowl. "I'm struggling to wrap my head around everything that's happened. Every time things start to settle into something resembling normal, life takes another twist, and I'm off balance again."

That I was surprised by David's response said more about me than it did about him. There was nothing sexual in the way his arms came around me, only a sense of comfort and understanding that made me come undone. When tears gathered in the corners of my eyes, I let them fall.

"I'm here. Let it all out. You'll feel better if you do." His voice, deep and soothing, unlocked the storm of emotions inside me, and I let them spill out in cleansing sobs.

He held me and patted my back until my breath stopped hitching, and then gently let me go.

"Thanks." Feeling awkward, I stepped away and tried to read his expression. "I should say I'm sorry for soaking your shoulder, but I won't. I needed a good cry more than I realized."

David shrugged off the moment and nudged past me to pull open the refrigerator door. "Feed me, and we'll call it even." He pulled out a carton of eggs and set them near the stove. "Do you believe in redemption?"

The question sounded like the opening of the conversation I'd been waiting to have. Finally, I would get to hear what had brought this man into my parent's home and into my life.

"I believe in fresh starts enough to raise money to foster them, so yeah, I do."

He settled in at the table, waiting while I folded cheese and chopped peppers into the eggs, and then made them into omelets.

"I'm listening if you want to tell me about yours," I said as soon as we'd tucked in.

The pause that followed was cut short by the strident sound of my ring tone coming from the bedroom. "I'm sorry. I should answer that." With everything going on, it was probably more bad news. David nodded, and I ran to pick up before it went to voicemail.

"Where are you?" Robin's strident tone made me cringe and hold the phone away from my ear. "Aren't you coming to the office?"

"I assumed ... you know, with Spencer dead—"

She cut me off. "I need you. Hurry up and get here. Park around back and bring your key."

"I ... okay. I'll be right there. I just need—" Too late. She'd hung up. I did the same and just stared at my phone for a moment before returning to the kitchen, where David was feeding the last bite of his omelet to the dog.

"I'm sorry. I guess I have to go to work."

"So I heard." Rising, David gathered his plate and took it to the sink. "Finish eating first. There's nothing so urgent that you have to skip breakfast. I'll clean up and take Molly out for a good long walk before I finish mowing the lawn."

When I merely stared at him, he offered, "It's okay, when I asked about redemption, I didn't mean from a life of crime. You can trust me. I've known where your key is for weeks now, and I haven't shown up to pillage the place, have I?"

But I'd wanted to hear his story, and now there wasn't time. "Raincheck on that talk we were about to have?"

He nodded. "Done."

"Okay, thanks again for everything. You know, I am capable of riding a mower. You don't have to keep taking care of me even if you do feel some sort of obligation to my folks."

A flash of annoyance crossed his face and then was gone. "I like mowing lawns. There's a certain amount of Zen for me in the work. Would you begrudge me a little peace of mind, or can we just call it a friendly gesture? I'd like to be friends."

Defeated by his logic, I waved a hand toward the window. "Have at it, then." I gave him a genuine smile.

49

If I trusted my father's judgment, and he trusted David implicitly, how could I do less?

In ten minutes, I'd eaten, dressed hastily, and was on my way to the office.

CHAPTER 7

The woman waiting for me bore no resemblance to either the one I'd been working with for the past few weeks or the tragic figure from the grocery store the day before. Gone was the flawless makeup, wad of chewing gum, and blank stare; gone was the puddle of tears over the loss of her one true love. This Robin looked like she'd slept under a bush or been dragged through one.

When I walked toward her, she snapped her fingers for me to hurry.

"Good, you're here. Quick, unlock the door."

"Don't you have your own keys?" We weren't here to work; something else was going on.

Leftover traces of lip dye stood out starkly against a face gone sheet-white except for where the blue mascara she favored made bruise-colored rings around her eyes. The hand she used to push her hair back quivered like an aspen leaf ahead of a storm.

"The police think I killed Spencer." I'd just slid the key into the lock when the confession stopped me cold. I pulled the key back out and turned toward her.

"Did you kill him?" As if she'd confess, but the question flew out before I could clamp my lips down to stop it.

Robin's feet suddenly seemed interesting to her. "Not directly, but he might be dead because of something I did."

Hope surged at the prospect of being ghost-free again. "Tell me what you know."

"Oh, nothing in particular. I just thought it might be my fault because that cop came to my house last night."

Talking to Robin required a lot of deep breathing if I wanted to retain my composure. I whistled one in through my nose, then another before saying, "And you didn't ask him why he was there?"

51

"I thought he was going to arrest me, so I went out the back, and now I'm on the run from the law. You have to help me prove I'm innocent."

It would be easier than proving she had more than half a brain. "Let me get this straight—you think Spencer is dead because of something you may or may not have done, you're scared of talking to the police, and your first thought was to essentially break into his office to prove you didn't kill him?"

Robin looked at me like I had asked her the square root of pi. "No. I left my best pair of shoes in the office, and I wanted to get them before I leave town."

I hoped the throbbing in my left temple wasn't an early sign of an aneurysm, though if it was, I wouldn't have been surprised. Robin snatched the key from my hand and practically shoved me down the steps in her haste to fit it in the lock.

"Looking for more bodies, Everly?" Ernie Polk's voice was a cold-shower shock. Robin jumped, dropped my keys down between the steps and the wall, and raised her hands in the air.

"Don't shoot," she wailed. "I surrender."

"There go my car keys." This day just got better and better as Ernie approached. "Put your hands down, you fool." It wasn't like he had his gun out or anything.

"I don't look for them, they just seem to find me," I replied to Ernie's question. It was useless to argue, though. In the two months since I'd been home, I'd found two bodies. It certainly didn't look good.

Robin let out a wail and crumpled to sit on the steps. "Go ahead, I know you're here to arrest me." Her voice sounded muffled since she'd dropped her head on her knees.

Ignoring her, I asked, "Did you find evidence that Spencer's death wasn't an accident after all?"

"No, just the opposite. We found proof it was an accident. Just like I said. " Ernie showed me his stern face. I gave him back an eyebrow raise. Since Spencer was still hanging around, there should have been some evidence of murder.

"Well, don't leave me in suspense."

"I'll spare you the gory details, but we found a tennis ball near the body," He paused when Robin let out another wail. "And the end of a dog leash over behind the operator's shed. Figured the dog got loose and Spencer was chasing her. Just really bad timing."

If only because I knew better, the story shot my BS meter up to ten.

"What about the alarm? Shouldn't he have some warning to get out of the way?"

Ernie looked away. "Neighbors complained about the noise at night, so Ron shut off the alarm during off-hours."

Frowning, I picked up on what would have been high irony if I didn't know better. "The only neighbors close enough to hear the alarm would be Spencer and whoever lives in the house next door. Can I assume he's the one who complained?"

Robin sniffled, and Ernie nodded. "He said it bothered the dog. But, it was an accident, pure and simple." That settled, he looked down at Robin. "Is there a reason why I should arrest you, Miss Stafford?"

Robin's head came up, and for the first time, I felt bad instead of merely annoyed with her for being such a ditz.

"No, I didn't do anything wrong. Why did you come to my house?" Standing, Robin brushed her hands down her backside as if to smooth her clothes, then she squared her shoulders and rubbed her palms across her cheeks to clear away the moisture left from tears. Mostly she managed to smear away the rest of the leftover makeup, but even that was an improvement.

Over her head, I caught a glimpse of Ernie's face as it reddened. "I ... uh ... when I was going through his personal effects, I found a photo of you in his wallet." He cleared his throat. "It was not the kind of photo you want just anyone to see."

When he pulled it out of his pocket, I caught a flash of naked Robin.

"On that note"—I knelt and reached between the steps to try and retrieve my keys—"I'll just head on home."

"No. Please don't." Robin pleaded. "Now that we're here, we could go in, clear our things out, and take care of the office. That's okay, isn't it?" She tucked the compromising photo into her back pocket and waited for Ernie's ruling on the matter.

"We'll need to notify his clients and the mortgage companies," I added.

Ernie thought about it for a moment. "I guess it's okay. We've notified his next of kin. Bad blood between them, if you ask me. She didn't seem too broken up at the news."

"I just need to get my keys first." I could see the ring if I peered under the steps, but not quite reach them.

"Let me." Ernie heaved a sigh and gently eased me out of the way. Since giving back the picture, he hadn't made eye contact with Robin at all, but I decided she couldn't be too heartbroken over Spencer if she was already looking at another man's butt that way.

I wanted to remind her Ernie was at least ten years too old for her and married besides, but I clamped my lips shut and pretended I hadn't seen a thing.

"Where should we start?" My question appeared to catch Robin off guard, and I wondered if she suffered some form of short-term memory loss. "Should we notify clients first, or contact the underwriters? Is there another broker in the area who could finish up the current contracts?"

Robin shrugged and went into the supply closet. I heard rustling and then she emerged with an empty box which she began to fill with the contents of her desk. Mostly magazines and bottles of nail polish. *Take care of the office* meant something different to her than it did to me.

"Okay, then. I'll just—" Quit wasting my breath and use this chance to look for a clue that might lead to Spencer's killer. Robin didn't even notice when I went into his office instead of my own.

Of course, his computer required a password.

"Psst. Spencer. Show yourself."

Hey, what do you want from me? If there was any such thing as proper haunting protocol, no one ever told me.

"Now would be a good time to pop in. I could use your help."

In the utter silence that followed, I tried the most obvious password option and typed in M-O-L-L-Y. Hitting enter rewarded me with the welcome screen. Spencer was a hacker's dream come true.

First things first, I logged into the email account to check the status on all open accounts and found the first piece of information that might lead anywhere. Sometime during the afternoon before he'd been killed, Spencer had sent a flurry of emails. As I read through those and the responses, I learned he'd called in favors

54

with the underwriters and title companies. Three of the four closings we'd had on the books for the month were now marked clear to close. All I needed to do was make a few calls to break the bad news and ask the mortgage companies to send someone to take his place at the signings.

The fourth folder, the one containing Cassidy Chandler's documentation, was missing, and ten minutes of searching only proved it was gone off the network as if it had never existed.

Maybe Robin would know something.

I snorted. Who was I kidding?

Then I remembered Spencer telling me he planned to refer her to another lending institution. The something fund ... or somesuch funding. I drew a blank on the name and had to close my eyes to dredge it up from the depths of my memory.

Quantum Funding. That was it.

I ran a new search, and that one came up empty, too.

At a loss for what to do next, I put my newly acquired, if less than stellar, lock-picking skills to the test, and with a bent paper clip, jimmied Spencer's top desk drawer. If he didn't want me looking through his stuff, he should have crossed over when he had the chance. But no, he had to haunt me, so I felt no remorse for snooping.

"Thank you, YouTube," I muttered when the lock on the top drawer popped open.

Looking at the contents, I wondered if Spencer and Catherine were related. Why would he feel the need to lock up a half a dozen pens, a stapler, and the instruction booklet for the printer?

Run into a lot of stapler thieves, did he?

I moved the booklet aside and hit pay dirt with an envelope addressed by hand to Spencer at the office. Curious, I drew out the single sheet and read the first few lines that were written in dark, slashing penmanship.

Someone had been unhappy with Spencer. So unhappy, in fact, that they threatened him with bodily harm if he didn't *stop dicking around with me and my family's future.* Ernie Polk would have to eat crow once he saw these. Even better, Spencer could fly off into the ether where he belonged and leave me alone.

I tucked the letter into my purse. As much as I wanted to prove Ernie wrong, I wasn't about to make a fool of myself, so I planned to do a little investigating on my own before I handed over the evidence.

A few minutes later, the phone rang, and I should have known when Robin didn't pick up that she'd left without so much as a goodbye, but I checked anyway and answered on the third ring.

"Spencer Charles' office, Everly speaking."

"Who's this?"

"It's Everly Dupree, can I help you, Mr. Hanson?" I'd recognized his voice even before scanning the readout on the phone's ID screen.

"Let me talk to Spencer."

Sigh. "I'm sorry, Leo. I thought you'd have heard by now. There was an accident, and Spencer was killed. I'm so sorry."

There was a short pause, and then, "Don't that beat all. Well, I guess that's why he hasn't been answering his phone. Dead, you say? Since when?"

Leo didn't sound overly broken up about the prospect.

"Since yesterday. I'd have thought the news would be over town by now." And I knew for a fact that Leo visited the diner for his daily cup of coffee and to ogle the owner. The only person in town who didn't know he harbored a secret crush for her was Mabel herself. "Didn't you hear about it at the diner this morning?"

"Well, that changes a few things." Leo acted like he didn't hear the question. "Spencer was a good man; I'm awful sorry to hear he's dead." His sorrow, however, seemed short-lived. "You need to send a carpenter over to 116 Tulip Street to take a look at the porch railing. The renter's left at least a dozen messages. Don't know why she's calling me when I hired a perfectly good property manager to handle such things."

"You want me to arrange for the repairs?"

"Didn't I say that? Now how soon can you have someone on-site?"

I'd known Leo at least peripherally for half my life, and this was the first time I'd ever seen him as not so quick on the uptake.

"As I've said, Spencer is no longer with us." Well, that wasn't entirely true, since *us* included me, and while he wasn't technically with me at the moment...oh, you get the drift. "Which means he will no longer be able to provide you with property management services."

"You work for him, so why can't you take care of it, then?"

"Mr. Hanson, Spencer has passed on, I am no longer in his employ." It was a simple concept, right?

"Then why did you answer the phone?"

A valid question, I supposed. "I'm only here today to tie up any loose ends for our clients."

"That's fine. Consider the railing a loose end."

This conversation had turned into the verbal equivalent of a yo-yo. "Let me put this in terms you'll understand. I'm only here as a courtesy. With Spencer gone, there's no one left to pay me, so I don't actually work here anymore. Besides, what you're asking me to do was never part of my job description to begin with."

Leo sighed so hard I almost felt the wind of it over the phone.

"I'll pay you then. Problem solved. You need a job, and I need someone to send a guy over to 116 Tulip Street to look at a porch railing. What do you say? You want to be my new property manager?"

He named a weekly salary that was not that much less than my former pay. "You want it, the job's yours. How's a man supposed to enjoy his retirement with tenants calling at all hours of the day?"

"All hours of the day?"

Backtracking a little, Leo assured me the job wasn't all that difficult. I'd need to keep the units rented, handle maintenance calls, schedule repairs, and collect the rent at the first of the month. I could do all of that from home, and Leo didn't, as he assured me twice, give a hoot in hell if I worked another job as long as I kept the tenants off his back.

I might regret it later, but I said yes.

"Do you have any idea who Spencer used for maintenance?" The beep that signaled a hangup sounded before I got the whole sentence out, so I searched through Spencer's contact list for the name of a contractor or handyman.

Why was it that ghosts could drop into my life willy-nilly, but when I needed to ask a question, they were suddenly rarer than hen's teeth? At a loss, I turned to the one person I knew who might be able to help.

"David," I said when he answered his phone on the third ring. "How would you like to earn some extra cash?"

"We've had this discussion already. I won't take your money for a little mowing, and I'm happy to help out with Molly from time to time." He sounded offended, though I had begun to wonder if that was his baseline.

"It's not for me. I need someone to go over to 116 Tulip Street and take a look at a loose porch railing. I'll pay ten percent over the going rate if you can get over there in the next hour. It's a rental unit, and I'll spare you the gory details, but I've just become the property manager. I didn't know who else to call."

He paused so long I wondered if the line had gone dead.

"David? Can you hear me?"

"Okay. I'll do it." The tone of his voice sounded guarded. "Just give me a few minutes to get Molly settled, and I'll head right over."

"You're a lifesaver. Thank you! Do whatever you need to do to fix the railing and make the bill out to Leo Hanson. If you need materials, call me, and I'll make arrangements at the hardware store."

His assent sounded rushed, so I thanked him again and hung up to let him take care of the problem.

Not even a full day later, and I'd already replaced enough of my income to cover my living expenses. Out of tragedy, a measure of triumph. I congratulated myself.

One of these days, I will learn not to taunt the fates by thinking I had everything under control.

Today would not be that day.

CHAPTER 8

The place was eerily quiet.

Since Spencer had taken the time to put his work affairs in order, there wasn't anything more for me to do, so I decided to clean out my office. That took about three minutes and ended with a pitiful pile of belongings on my desk: a spare power cable for my phone and a box of granola bars. I hadn't spent enough time there to make it my second home.

I took one final look through the computer files in my former office hoping to find Cassidy's number when I remembered I'd used my phone to call her once. Her number was in my call log.

"Cassidy," I said when I heard her harried voice on the other end of the line. "This is Everly Dupree. We spoke on the phone the other day."

The slight edge of frustration gave way to a more guarded tone. "Yes, you worked with Spencer Charles. I heard the news about him. Such a tragic loss."

"It was. The reason for my call," I said as I braced myself for the inevitable verbal tirade, "is that I wanted to say I'm sorry Spencer wasn't able to push your mortgage through before he passed."

There was a second of silence, and then Cassidy said, "But I've already signed the papers. Didn't Spencer tell you? It was like a miracle the way he showed up here the night before last with the lawyer and the paperwork all ready to sign. I could hardly believe it even after he handed me the keys. I'm packing right now, and I still can't believe it's finally happening. My kids are going to have their own rooms."

"You signed the papers. Before he died," I repeated in shock. "Did he say anything about why the deal went through so suddenly?"

"No, he just called me and said he'd made the arrangements, and everything was all set, and if we did the paperwork right then, I could have the rest of the month to move in. If I'd have known what was going to happen to him, I'd have treated him nicer. I'm afraid I gave him a hard time for making me jump through so many hoops."

My mind struggled to catch up.

"Can you tell me the name of the lender?"

"Sure, I ought to remember since I saw it about half a million times on the paperwork. The name of the company is Quantum Funding. Why? Is there a problem. I've already signed the papers. You can't go back on the deal now."

"No, Cassidy, there's no problem. I'm so happy for you. Congratulations on your new home."

I wished her well before we hung up.

Whenever Spencer showed up again, I needed to find out why he'd hustled every deal through so quickly. Had he known someone was gunning for him?

Maybe he'd had some sort of premonition or something. How creepy would that have been? I supposed I could ask him the next time he bothered to show up. If he ever did. For all I knew, he'd crossed over into the light without saying goodbye.

Except I doubted he'd go without a final visit with Molly, so he was more likely choosing to stay away on purpose.

Or for another reason entirely as I learned after I locked up the office and started back toward home. Half a block away, he shivered into existence next to me.

"I could have used your help back there. What's the deal with not showing up? Or can you not hear me when I call?" I tried not to move my lips too much. All I needed now was to develop a reputation as Everly Dupree, the woman who walks around town talking to herself.

"Hey, not my fault. I tried, but I guess I'm not allowed in the office. That place is like a cosmic revolving door, because every time I went in, I ended up outside again."

"Wonderful," I let sarcasm coat my tongue even though the taste of it was bitter. "So very helpful."

Home now, I mounted the steps, unlocked the door, and went inside before unleashing my annoyance. "When you finally decide to cross over and leave me in peace, would you do me a favor?

Would you track down the sadistic jerk who decided my life wouldn't be complete without a few ghosts in it? And when you do, tell him or her or it, that it would help if they'd lighten up on the rules a little."

An ugly band of tension settled across my forehead when I got a look at Spencer's stubborn expression. Even if he could, he wasn't going to leave me in peace.

"Just go in there," I said, pointing toward the living room, "while I change and take something for this headache."

While I was at it, I made myself a sandwich and waited until the combination of food and painkillers kicked in. If I'd hoped to find Spencer duly chastised and ready to spill his every secret, I should have known I'd be doomed to disappointment. Molly sprawled across the sofa with her head sort of in his lap, and I mean *in* it. It was a weird thing to see and gave me the shivers, but she didn't seem to notice any ill effect from the contact.

Tossing the threatening letter on the table in front of him, I said, "What can you tell me about this?"

"There's nothing to tell. It's old news. Water under the bridge. Ancient history." Spencer paused.

"What? Run all out of clichés, did ya?"

He grinned. "I guess so, anyway, that letter is a non-issue. In my line of work, people tend to get emotional when things don't work out the way they hoped. Some of them find ways to vent. That's all the letter was. A dissatisfied client taking his frustration out on me."

The headache hadn't quite gone, and it threatened to come roaring on.

"Most frustrated people don't make death threats. There's no return address, so how do you even know who sent it?"

Spencer waved a dismissive hand. "I know. Let it go, Everly. You're looking in the wrong direction. Trust me."

"Fine." I huffed and shot my nose in the air, intending to do no such thing. "What made you push to close all the open cases so quickly? Was someone else threatening you?"

"No. Last month, I tried to get a reservation on a cabin rental up in Mackinaw, and they didn't have any openings, so when they called to tell me they'd had a cancellation for next week, I cleared my calendar."

61

My theory went down in flames. "Okay then, tell me about Quantum Funding."

With about the same amount of drama as when Dorothy tossed her bucket of water, Spencer went through his *vibrate, chill, and fade* sequence. Not two seconds later, the only one left on the sofa was Molly.

I shivered in the aftermath. "I should get him to do that more often so I can save on the air conditioning bill." The dog didn't see the humor in the observation. "Come on, Molly. Let's go find you a tennis ball."

CHAPTER 9

Leaping and twisting, Molly caught the tennis ball on the bounce and ran full tilt toward me for the return. Halfway back, she heard David's truck turn down the street and changed course to pass me and dance near the gate.

"You're ridiculous, you know that?" I couldn't hold back a smile at her antics. To David, when his booted feet hit the driveway, I said, "I think she likes you. Can you tell?"

"Dogs are usually good judges of character."

I popped the gate latch and watched Molly try to mow him down with enthusiasm. "You're just trying to get me to stroke your ego. I already admitted I rushed to judgment where you were concerned. Don't push your luck or I'll let my dog kiss you to death." Or not since he'd probably just end up haunting me if I did.

Grinning, he picked up the slobber-covered tennis ball and tossed it for Molly. "Porch rail's fixed over on Tulip."

"All joking aside, I can't tell you how much I appreciate you taking care of this for me." When he handed it to me, I looked at the low amount on the bill. "Ten bucks? This can't be right. What about materials?"

"Don't worry about it. Fifteen minutes and a couple of screws to anchor the post back down." He had on his *don't argue with me* face, so, for once, I didn't.

"Why's some guy playing with my dog?" Speaking of being haunted. "You didn't tell me you had a boyfriend."

"I don't." An indignant retort popped out before I could stop it. David turned to look at me quizzically, and I had to think fast to cover, "know if you've heard, but Molly was with Spencer when the accident happened. That's how she knew where to find him. Ernie thinks she's the reason he was in the recycling center outside of business hours. It's too bad she can't tell us what happened."

"Life's full of mysteries, and so are dogs. If you don't believe me, just look at her." David held the soggy ball while Molly spun. Three turns to the left, then three turns to the right.

"She does that sometimes. I have no idea why." I lied and directed a pointed look toward Spencer who shrugged and at least had the grace to look apologetic.

"Go play, Molly."

Once David's back was turned, Spencer said, "I'm not going to be much help. The last thing I remember before it happened is handing Cassidy Chandler a pen."

I wanted to ask if he thought she had anything to do with his death, but not in front of David, or even behind him as the case may be.

The third time Molly bypassed David to drop the ball at Spencer's feet, emotion overcame him, and he faded away. I covered by acting like it was my turn to throw the ball. David didn't seem to want to talk, so we threw the ball in silence until Molly was tired.

"You don't have to tell me about your painful past, and I'm truly sorry for treating you poorly. There's no excuse for the way I acted, and I won't offer one. Stay with my parents for as long as you need to." I laid a hand on David's arm and gave it a squeeze. "Friends?"

"Am I forgiven for the frog incident?"

The memory of the cold, wet frog scrabbling against my spine had lingered since the time my family had visited his in Vermont when I was young. I considered, and then said, "Don't push your luck. Give me another ten years, and we'll see. Or explain to my mother that you and I will not be dating, and we'll call it even."

He gave me a tentative smile, followed me inside, and settled at the table while I shuffled through containers of leftovers in the fridge. "I've got cold chicken. Want a sandwich?"

"Sure. Whatever you're having is fine."

As if he found it easier to talk to my back, David said, "I'd been living in my truck for nine months, two weeks, and four days when your father found me."

My hands paused in the act of placing pieces of chicken on slices of bread. "I had no idea." Now I felt even worse for the way

64

I'd treated him, and a little hurt that my parents had kept secrets from me. "Why didn't they tell me?"

"Partly because they were respectful of my privacy, and partly because there's a stigma to homelessness. People make assumptions."

I couldn't argue with that logic since I hadn't known even this much of his story, and I'd made a few myself, not in the way he meant, but then, so had he. I set the plates on the table, followed those with a couple of glasses, and pulled a pitcher of iced tea from the fridge to give myself time to think of what to say.

"You thought I'd judge you," I said as I filled our glasses then took a seat.

"Not just you, but I guess I did."

"And I played right into your worst expectations by acting the way I acted." I bit into my sandwich. "I'll own that, but I will point out that you underestimated me before I showed up and spectacularly proved your point."

David left his plate untouched. "I suppose that's true."

"It's enough to know we've put our differences behind us. It's okay to let the past lie if that's what it takes to move forward." Something I'd like to do myself if my ex didn't keep rearing his ugly head. By the end of David's story, I'd be grateful for my own demons. His had pointier teeth.

"Jeremy was my dorm mate during my second year at Penn State. Great guy, top of the class, made friends everywhere he went. The kind of guy who knew what he wanted out of life and had since he could remember. Jeremy was going to be a doctor, and a damn good one, but more, he was a good friend."

"You went to med school?"

The look he gave me was a clear warning to shut up, so I did. "By the end of the year, I realized I wasn't cut out for college life. I had the grades, I just didn't have the conviction it takes to complete years of study, so I changed paths, and became a certified paramedic. Dad tried to get me to move back to Vermont, but I'd met a girl, so I decided to stick around and took a job in Harrisburg."

Absently, David slid his glass of tea back and forth, but he never even took the first sip.

65

"I loved my job. The good, the bad, and even the ugly of it. Saving lives, helping people, delivering babies. It was never boring." His tone deepened, and I knew we were getting to the crux of the story.

"I was on duty when the call came in. It was supposed to be my night off, but I'd switched shifts with someone. I don't remember why. Anyway, the accident call came in, and we rolled out. Just two minutes away, we were the first on-scene."

The way David's eyes went unfocused, I knew he was reliving that night in his head, and I felt horrible for him.

"I knew at first glance it was going to be bad, but this was the worst I'd ever seen. Two vehicles. Head-on collision. The other driver walked away with minor injuries, but Jeremy's car was so twisted I didn't realize it was his until I heard him begging for help."

"Oh, David." I reached across the table to take his hand.

"Only two minutes, and we were still too late. I know that now, I knew it then, but I couldn't do the job. I couldn't remember what I needed to do to save him." We were both crying now. "I lied and told him it would be okay, that he would be okay. They had to pull me away, but he was already gone."

Saying I'm sorry often seems like far too little and too late, but it was all I had to offer, and I meant it with every cell in my body.

"I walked away from the job that night, and after the funeral, I walked away from my life. I packed a few things, got in my truck, and kept driving. When your dad found me, I'd been gone so long I didn't know how to come back. It took another month, and plenty of patience on his part, before I came around to thinking I might be able to live among people again."

My heart broke for him. "You asked me if I believed in redemption. If you think you need to atone for anything, you're wrong. You comforted your friend in the only way you could at the time. I don't know if it's true, but I think our loved ones watch over us once they've passed. Don't you wonder if his was the guiding hand that helped my father find you and bring you home?"

It was my turn to hold him while he cried, and to hope he'd feel cleaner when it was done. He seemed lighter somehow when he sat back down to finally eat his chicken sandwich.

"Sorry about sending you over to fix that porch railing. Does it bother you to be around people still?" He'd helped Momma Wade with landscaping, and I'd seen him at the hardware store, so he wasn't a total hermit. "It seemed like you didn't want to go at first, and I realize now I steamrollered right over you."

When he grinned, he was so handsome I wished he was the one to make my heart go pitter-pat.

"It wasn't anything like that. Don't worry about it." He changed the subject. "I see you didn't get too far with the painting project in here."

"No, you were right." His eyes lit up at the admission. "That wallpaper eats primer for lunch. I can't even imagine what it would do to the steamer. I've been looking at wallpaper books. I figure if you can't beat 'em, join 'em."

"Go down to the hardware store tomorrow and ask Tim to show you some samples of the paintable paper. I think it's just the thing you're looking for."

Confession time over, he ruffled Molly's head and said he'd see me next week when it was time to mow again. This time, I didn't argue.

67

CHAPTER 10

"This is stupid." Talking to Molly had become a habit already, and as I tested each key in the addition door for the tenth time, she sat and watched. "Why wouldn't she have put the key to this door on the ring with the rest? It doesn't make sense."

That was the crux of the problem. Just basing my opinions off what I'd found in the house so far, I couldn't get enough of a handle on Catherine's state of mind to figure out where she might have stashed the key. So far, I had a list of places it wasn't, but that hadn't helped me narrow down the location.

If I had to be haunted, I'd have preferred Catherine's ghost to Hudson's or Spencer's. The picture I was getting of her through sorting out her things made me wish I'd had a chance to know the woman. If for no other reason than to ask her where she'd hidden that key.

"Okay, I'm Catherine Willowby." Molly cocked her head at me. "I take the time to stack games into a cabinet and notebooks into a drawer so tightly they fit like puzzle pieces." Ooh, that sparked something. "Puzzles. I like puzzles, fitting things together, making sense out of chaos." And still, there had been a stack of paper crowns on a shelf in the kitchen and a closet full of mannequin heads upstairs. How did those fit with what else I knew about Catherine?

"I throw great Halloween parties, so I'm whimsical and outgoing, but I keep all the rooms locked, so I'm either closed-off or hiding something. My car is meticulously detailed, so I'm particular. I like to sit in my tower room with a pair of binoculars. Nosy."

While I considered, I wound my way through the downstairs rooms with Molly following so closely, her nose stayed pressed against the back of my leg. Maybe I was over-thinking. She had organized her kitchen cabinets and drawers with utility in mind. Sure, no one needed fifteen spatulas, but they were right where I wanted them when I was cooking.

Other than tossing out half the contents of her junk drawer and making space for what few things I had of my own, I'd left that room pretty much as I'd found it because everything felt so comfortable and right.

If we shared kitchen preferences to the point where I could reach absently for a pot or pan and find it in the exact right place, maybe all I needed to do was stop thinking and reach for the key to the addition.

Yeah, I know how it sounded, and that Momma Wade would have had a field day if she caught me trying to channel the dead, but I figured it was worth a shot, so I tried. Blanking my mind of anything other than my intent to open that door, I marched down the hall and reached for the most natural spot to find the key—the drawer on the front of a rounded table set into a shallow alcove just past the kitchen door.

How many times had I walked right by this spot and glanced at the pretty, enameled vase sitting on the tabletop?

My breath caught, and my heart kicked up a little speed. The key had to be here because this felt so right. And then, as my fingers brushed against the polished wood, that glowing burst of triumph popped like a soap bubble. There was no knob, and given the smooth surface below the tabletop, no drawer, either.

Molly's toenails scrabbled against the floor when I huffed out a couple of curse words in a louder voice than I'd intended.

"I'm sorry, girl. Come here." Squatting, I coaxed her with an apology in soothing tones. "I didn't mean to scare you." As a reward, she tried to climb into what she perceived as my lap and sent me over. "Good thing I was already most of the way down." Laughing, I turned my head to avoid a slobbering kiss, and from that angle, noticed something odd about the underside of the table.

Shoving Molly gently back, I sat up and scooted over enough to get a good look at the unmistakable outline of the bottom of a drawer. I tugged at the lower edge of the front panel, and it didn't even wiggle.

"Now, how does this thing open?" Molly dropped to her haunches to watch while I poked and prodded. "Maybe it's spring-loaded." I pushed against what I took to be the drawer front, and other than nearly tipping over the vase, nothing happened. "Guess not."

Determined to learn the secrets of the table, I moved the vase to the living room for safety and headed out to the garage to retrieve a few tools. As soon as I opened the door, Molly shot through it.

"Molly," I called after her, but she'd gone out of sight before I hit the porch. Sighing, I turned back for her leash and my car keys.

Back on the porch, I caught a glimmer out of the corner of my eye, so I didn't jump when Spencer popped into sight. "It's okay, she's in the backyard. You don't have to worry, she's not usually one to run off."

"So you say, but that doesn't explain how she ended up here the day you—" I broke off when I got a look at his face. "I'm an idiot. Molly didn't show up on my doorstep at random. You brought her here, didn't you?"

"Took you long enough to figure it out. I'm not liking your odds of finding out who killed me."

"Okay, then. You have a nice trip into the light. Don't let the veil hit you in the ass on your way out." Good riddance to him if he didn't want my help. Walking right through him wasn't the smartest thing I could have done, but it got my point across. By the time he got himself back together, I was in the backyard gearing up to lob a slobber-coated tennis ball while Molly danced in anticipation. "You really do have the most deplorable people skills."

"I'm sorry, I always morph into my father when I'm under stress."

"That is not an apology, it's an excuse." The ball thwacked wetly against the strings of the old racket, and Molly churned up the ground in her haste to get ahead and catch the fuzzy, yellow orb before it came back to earth.

"It's not even a very good excuse. I didn't ask you to drag your afterlife into my present one. How am I supposed to track down your killer? It's not like I have a way to narrow down the suspects. You managed to piss off everyone you knew at one time or another."

"I know," he said. "I was a jerk and probably deserved to die." There was an edge of sarcasm to his tone.

"No you didn't, but the last time I tried to help a ghost, I nearly ended up becoming one myself. I don't have any interest in repeating that performance, so you need to back off and give me some space."

Molly dropped her ball at his feet, and he automatically bent to pick it up. Annoyed as I was, I felt sorry for him when his hand passed right through, and I saw the wash of sadness at not being able to play with the dog.

Why? Why did he have to show me his soft spots?

"I said I'd help you," I sighed and used the racket to drag the ball toward me. I hadn't fully warmed up from the chill of walking through him, so I wasn't getting that close again. "But unless you can dredge up more helpful information, you're just going to have to let me figure things out in my own time and my own way."

The air chilled and shook with the force of Spencer's will as he tried again to give me something helpful.

"Hey." The tennis racket shot out of my hand and halfway across the yard.

Fading from the effort, Spencer tossed another apology at me along with a half garbled sentence. I caught the words computer and office.

Her tongue lolling sideways, panting from her efforts, Molly sidled up against my leg as if for reassurance she wasn't alone. I petted her sleek head, and she only looked back once before she followed me inside. She split off to slurp up half the water in her dish while I tried to remember what I'd been doing before the ghostly interruption.

Oh, right. The drawer.

Would Catherine keep the key to half her house in a drawer that needed tools to open? Probably not.

"There has to be something I'm missing." I can tell you I was talking to Molly, but she wasn't even in the room, so yeah, I was talking to myself, and to make it worse, I talked to the table, too. "How do you open?"

Since the table declined to answer, I pulled it gently out of the alcove for a better look. Small and sturdily built, it weighed more than I expected. Still, without much more than a gentle yank, it popped out into the middle of the hall on feet that looked like claws holding glass marbles, and I heard items rattling around in the drawer.

The drawer that wouldn't open no matter what I tried. Pushing from the back, pulling on the front, lifting the tabletop. Nothing worked. "Where was this thing made? Fort Knox?"

Finally, after I grabbed the flashlight from the kitchen, I spotted a tiny button that had blended into the decorative carving at the top of the curved leg. "Gotcha," I said and gave it a push. I felt the button give, heard a little pinging sound, and sucked in a breath when some hidden spring pushed the drawer open.

I won't deny it—I did a butt-wiggling two-step dance down the hallway before examining the contents. A stack of letters tied with a pink ribbon and a few newspaper clippings that I set aside to look at later, and sure enough, there was a key.

A brass key with an oval bow that I wasted no time fitting to the addition door. It slid in like a hot knife through butter and turned with a soft click. I'd worked myself up into quite a state imagining what lurked on the other side of that door. Enough that my pulse kicked up when I turned the knob and let the door swing wide.

CHAPTER 11

I'm not sure what I expected to find, but it wasn't something straight out of Wonderland with a wrong turn through Whoville. One thing was for certain—the new section was not a mirror image of the main house. Unless you were talking a funhouse mirror addition, and then you'd be right on the money.

In the main house, Catherine had hidden the evidence of her collector's sensibilities by stuffing every cabinet and drawer full to the brim. You had to look beneath the neat and tidy facade to see hints of her personality.

Not so in the newer section. Here, she'd let herself fly free. I only needed to see the first room to know this was where the woman with the closet full of mannequin heads had really lived.

In the room to my left, rough shelves made from boards and stacked wooden crates marched from one end to the other. Muted light filtered through the shaded windows to spark jewel-colored highlights off the contents: glass plates, bowls, candy dishes, figurines.

With a vision of Molly's tail wreaking havoc, I pushed the door closed behind me, hit the bank of light switches, and just stood taking in the rest of the space. If a second-hand shop and a recycling center had a mad affair and somehow managed to spawn a love child, this is where it would go to live.

When the lights came on, the great mannequin mystery was solved. The torsos that went with the closet full of heads hung from the rafters. Each one had been painted or collaged in some way, with can lights set into the arm and leg holes.

A giggle bubbled up and, knowing Jacy would never forgive me for doing otherwise, I texted her.

Found key, mystery rooms are open.

Two seconds later, she replied:

On my way, wait for me. I mean it. You wait.

Since the day was warm, I waited for her on the porch while Molly sniffed the hostas planted along the side of the garage. She barked once when she heard the Jeep slow and turn down Lilac Street, then lumbered over to sit at my feet.

"Next time some homicidal maniac shows up to try and kill me, I bet you'll be better protection than a ghost."

Maybe I wasn't being fair to the ghost of my high school sweetheart; he had saved me, but he'd also been the one to put me in the position of nearly being killed, so I guess it balanced out. His wife, Neena, lived right across the street, and we were on the way to becoming friends after a little bit of a rocky start.

Not long after the funeral, her car had disappeared from the driveway. Someone was keeping the lawn mowed, but I hadn't seen signs of life for at least three weeks. Rumor had it she'd gone home for a visit and hadn't decided whether to come back.

As soon as Jacy stepped out of the Jeep, I let go of Molly's collar. Not because I wanted to, but because she'd have dragged me off the porch if I didn't.

Legs akimbo, Molly dashed toward the newcomer. "No. Down." Voice firm, Jacy pointed a finger toward the ground, and the dog obeyed. "Still no sign of Neena?" She must have seen me looking toward the house.

"How do you do that? Are you like some magic dog whisperer?"

Grinning, Jacy bent to give the dog a good rub behind her ears, and said, "Dogs just need a firm word, and whatever you say to them, you need to mean it."

"This is Molly. I didn't get a chance to tell you about her the other day. She belonged to Spencer, and what with everything that happened, I couldn't let her go to the pound."

"Oh, poor thing. Are you keeping her? I think it would be good for you. Do you know how old she is?"

Taking the questions in order, I said, "Yes, she's mine unless a family member wants her, but so far, no one has even asked. I don't think Spencer and his family were close. She's not even a year old yet."

"Not much more than a puppy, but look how good she is. She wants to please, she just doesn't always remember what that means.

All it takes is a firm voice and lots of gentle reminders until she learns."

"You're going to be such a good mom. How's the peanut? Did Brian cry when you told him?"

She waved the question away. "He's a basket case, but in a good way. Now, enough about all of that. I want to see what's behind the mystery door."

What could I say to prepare her? Nothing she'd believe, so I opted for watching her face when she got a good look.

"Come on then." I led her inside.

"Whoa," Jacy froze, and her mouth dropped open. "This is … It's …" a fluttering of her hand indicated speechlessness.

"I know. It defies explanation."

"Wow," she finally said. "Just wow."

Essentially one large, open space with a second-floor loft, Catherine had used whatever came to hand to close off various sections into rooms. Folding screens separated the room full of glass from the next. Beyond that was a section walled off by grommeted canvas stretched between hooks screwed into the floor and the beams below the loft. If you squinted, you could almost see a loose sense of organization to the sheer volume of stuff crammed into the space.

Behind the canvas wall, we found a small pottery-making setup with a wheel, a kiln, and a single shelf holding some finished pieces. The way Catherine had arranged them, the series of hand-thrown mugs reminded me of those charts showing the evolution of man. They started out wonky-looking with uneven thicknesses on the sides and glopped-on handles. From left to right, each mug looked better than the last. The one on the end was a thing of beauty from the gracefully curved sides glazed a peacock blue, to the ornamental handle done in gold.

From somewhere behind me, Jacy said, "This place is unbelievable. You know what you bought, don't you?"

I had my own ideas, but I wanted to hear her take on it. "What?"

Her grin was wide, her eyes twinkling as she stepped beside me. "What you've got here is a mullet house."

"I don't follow."

75

"This house is like a mullet." Taking my arm in hers, she spun me around and pointed toward the hallway. "Old lady in the front, boho art chick meets junk collector in the back. I'd have liked to know Catherine, I think. It looks like she had a lot more going on than people realized. Did you ask your mom about any of this yet?"

"Right after I texted you, I called and asked her to stop by on her way home from work. I don't think she knew, or she'd have warned me. She would, right? All anyone ever says about Catherine is she lived alone and threw fantastic parties. I think if people knew all this was back here, they'd have said something, you know? Like *Catherine ... yeah, she was a nice old lady. Threw great parties, hung painted torso lights from the ceiling.* Seems like that would have rated at least one comment."

A few steps ahead of me now, Jacy whirled and said, "I bet no one knew, and it's like she had this secret life."

"Someone had to know. Look over there." I pointed to an area where furniture stacked three levels high in spots. "She couldn't have lifted any of that by herself, and she sure as heck didn't haul that table here in her car."

Lost in the what of it all, Jacy seemed uninterested in the why or the how. Then again, she wasn't the one responsible for sorting through and disposing of the mess. Resigned, I followed her up the metal steps to the window-lined loft.

"Oh, my." Jacy's breathy comment probably didn't bode well for me.

I gave her a gentle shove to get her moving again. "Budge up. I want to see."

She did, and I stepped into a workroom and studio that, compared to the chaos below, was ruthlessly organized. A pair of largish skylights cast sunlight over the painting resting on the easel below. My breath stilled.

In the painting, a spread-winged angel stood on a riverbank, cradling a woman to his chest. White hair flowed over his arm, and her eyes were closed, her face as pale as the shroud that covered her body.

Fine brush strokes captured sorrow in the tear beading on an eyelash, but also the measure of joy in his smile as he gazed down at the still face. It was almost as if she'd painted him in the act of

76

taking a breath because there was a sense of waiting, or maybe it was yearning. I couldn't be certain.

Overwhelmed, I sniffled.

"What's wrong?"

I pointed to the angel's face. "That's Mr. Willowby. There were photos of him on the walls when I moved in, remember?" The painting represented Catherine's most desperate wish to be reunited with her husband and for his to be the arms that carried her into the afterlife.

It was the saddest, most poignant thing I'd ever seen, and deeply personal.

"Where do you think she got all her money? She must have had thousands tied up in all this stuff. Do you remember when my mother went on that ceramics kick? She was going to buy a kiln and some molds off a guy advertising in the Northern Observer, but it would have cost the same as buying a used car, so daddy put his foot down. That was one of the few fights I remember them ever having."

"I'll have to ask my mother if she has any idea." I talked to Jacy's back as she peeled back the lid of one of several boxes piled in a corner. "What's in there? Anything good?"

Jacy turned to show me what she'd found. "These are cigar boxes, I think, with scenes painted on them. Just look at this one, with the sun setting over the water. I love the colors."

"Take it, it's yours."

"Thank you, I will." Jacy cradled the box to her chest, and I followed her back down the stairs. "But you're right, hoarding habits like this don't come cheap. Still, I think it must have been exciting to come into these rooms and pour her soul into creating art."

"Or sad because she had to hide her truest, most expressive self away where no one could see." Like I'd had to do with Paul to a lesser degree.

When she darted around a partition, Jacy's voice came back faintly. "I suppose we'll never know how she really felt."

Sadly, I suspected she was right.

Moving on to a new topic, Jacy said, "With a little work, you could make this into a cozy living space. You could have your bedroom up in the loft, add bathrooms up and down. Kitchen goes over there, with dining space in a nice, open floor plan."

"Why on earth would I need a second kitchen? Or another bedroom?"

"I don't know. I guess I was thinking you could live back here if you decided to do something with the main house. Or, you could turn this into a rental unit. Seems a shame not to do something with so much space."

I promised to think about the possibilities, but that was as far as I was willing to go. Mostly, I was tempted to close the door, lock it back up, and pretend the addition didn't exist.

CHAPTER 12

I saw the little folding sign for the dog training class just as I was beginning to think I was in the wrong place even though there was only one park in town. I expected to find a slew of owners tugging on the leashes of their unwieldy dogs but instead encountered a stern-looking Christine Polk—now Christine Murray—standing in front of a small group. All of whom, by the way, appeared to be seasoned professionals, if the serene expressions on their—and their dog's—faces were any indication.

It might have been more prudent of me to have listened when Christine suggested I wait for the start of a new session instead of inserting myself into the fourth week of a six-week course, but I needed to start out right with Molly, and I didn't want to waste time.

If she responded to me half as well as the other dogs did to their owners after only a couple of classes, I'd do my happy dance.

"Hello, Everly." Christine greeted me with what could only be described as half a smile. "And this must be Molly?" Judging by her mile-wide grin when she reached down to pat Molly's head, she cared more for dogs than she did humans. Probably not the worst trait for a dog trainer to have.

I think Christine expected every dog to take to her immediately, but Molly wasn't having any of that. She wrapped her leash around my legs in an attempt to get behind me, and then shoved her nose right into my butt.

"Sit, Molly," I commanded, attempting to replicate my mother's authoritative tone. She let out a little whine but sat, her tail wagging encouragingly, and I hoped it meant she'd already come to trust me and that training would be a piece of cake.

"She's quite skittish. That tells me she hasn't been properly socialized," Christine admonished, obliterating my hopeful mood. As if I'd had anything to do with Molly's training up until now.

"Have a seat, and follow along with the others. You've missed quite a lot of important information, so it might be best if you merely observed for today." I started to open my mouth and remind her I'd only been Molly's owner for a couple of days, but a sudden, vivid memory of Christine from grade school swam up from the depths.

We must have been nine or ten years old—I couldn't remember exactly— when Jacy's mother decided to surprise her by getting a kitten. She picked us up from school and drove out to the Polk's farm to let Jacy pick out the one she wanted from a litter one of the barn cats had dropped in the back of one of the stalls.

Mrs. Polk couldn't have been nicer. She took us out to look at the kittens, and along the way, showed us the right way to feed carrots to the horses. I remember shivering in awe as I felt the horse's lips brush against my palm, and the velvet softness of her nose when she nuzzled me for more.

When it was time to pick out a kitten, Christine waited for us inside the stall. Tall even at twelve or thirteen, she was all knees and elbows folded into the narrow space, with kittens practically hanging off her. Her mother told Jacy and me to go on in.

"Let the girls play with the kittens, Chris. Maybe you can help Jacy pick just the right one to take home."

At the time, I only had eyes for the balls of fluff with pink tongues and huge eyes, and I wanted nothing more than to take one home myself. Eager for a kitten cuddle if that was all that was on offer, I followed Jacy in and plunked down on the hay-covered floor.

Mrs. Polk and Momma Wade moved off a little way and started talking about whatever it was that women talked about in those days. I couldn't say, because a darling little tuxedo kitten had deserted Christine to climb into my lap.

"You're not getting that kitten." Christine raked an annoyed glare over me. "That one is mine, and he likes me better than you."

I thought he liked me just fine considering the way he'd curled up against my chest, buried his face in my neck, and was purring like he belonged there. Since I knew I wasn't getting a kitten that day, I didn't argue with her, so she turned and gave Jacy the same treatment over a precious little silky-haired bundle of gray fur.

Being Jacy, she met aggression with understanding. "I know she'll miss you, but I promise to take good care of her."

"You won't. No one can love her like I can. I'll hate you forever if you take her away from me."

Whether Christine would have said or done more, the mothers had returned.

"Is that the one you want?" Momma Wade asked Jacy, who gulped and nodded. A lot of the shine had gone off her day. "Bring her along then." Then she turned to me and repeated the question.

My heart raced as hope flared, and then died. "But, I'm not getting a kitten. I didn't ask permission, and my mother would kill me."

"Then it's a good thing I talked to her ahead of time."

I didn't even care that I'd landed on Christine's hate list, which I had. But with her mother standing close, she had to content herself with a withering glare. The same withering glare she had on her face now.

My face reddened, and I beat a hasty retreat toward a group of chairs set up in a U-shape, alternately tugging Molly along with me or being pulled behind her. Leash obedience was definitely our number-one priority. The other dog owners looked on, some with sympathy and others with barely concealed irritation at Molly's inability to sit still.

"This is Everly and Molly, everyone," Christine explained. "They'll be joining us for the rest of the session." One little pug stared at Molly, his curly tail vibrating as his front paws twitched with the effort of staying still. "Good boy, Brutus," his owner cooed as he reached down and deposited a tiny treat into the dog's mouth. Right then, I realized I'd forgotten the treats Christine had instructed me to bring and was suddenly grateful for my order to watch rather than participate.

While she waxed on about how consistency was the key to proper dog training, I took a moment to observe the group and discover there was some truth to the theory of dogs and owners looking alike.

One woman, who was clearly lost somewhere around 1985, sported a teased-to-perfection hairdo that had to have taken at least a half a can of Aquanet to achieve, and bore a striking resemblance to her Bichon Frise. To her left stood a round-headed balding man with a set of ears that were nearly the size and shape of his little French Bulldog, and I had to turn my head to keep from laughing

81

out loud at a poodle owner with a gravity-defying perm. It was too bad Jacy hadn't come along with me, although if she had, I'd probably never be allowed to return to class.

"It's time for this week's lesson," Christine said, pacing in front of the group. "You all seem to be doing quite well with the 'stay' command, but now it's time to tackle 'come' with distractions. Fortunately for us, we have a perfect distraction in the form of Molly here." She turned to me. "That is if Everly doesn't mind acting as my assistant." What choice did I have but to agree? That's right, none, and so I did.

About halfway through the class, I realized that whatever animosity Christine Murray had held onto over the decades-old kitten incident was now being loosed onto me whether I deserved the bulk of it or not. While the others, a long lead stretched between dog and owner, practiced commanding their pups to return to their sides, I was forced to run back and forth across the lawn until my lungs burned. Molly played her role well, yipping and pouncing playfully at me while the rest of the dogs looked on with excitement.

"Brutus! No!" The pug, sensing a moment of weakness, lunged away from his owner and came bounding up to Molly, sniffing her behind in a friendly hello that Molly did not appear to appreciate. She tried to get behind me, once again tangling her leash around my legs. I blew out a frustrated sigh. "See, it's not so fun when you're on the receiving end, is it, girl?" I murmured and gave the spot behind her silky ears a rub. She leaned into my hand and looked at me with those puppy dog eyes until I wanted to kick myself for forgetting the treats.

"Here, take this," the pug's owner said kindly and deposited a nugget of pepperoni-flavored meat stick into my hand. "Brutus seems to suffer from a bit of spatial dissonance; he seems to think he's a big tough guy, and he loves to play with other dogs."

I smiled and gestured toward Molly. "Same here, except the opposite. She's almost as big as I am, but she thinks she can sit on my lap. I heard it gets better with age."

"I certainly hope you're right. I worry he'll bite off more than he can chew one of these days. I'm Andy, by the way. Welcome to class."

"Thanks, but I think I might bow out after this one, come back and start at the beginning when the next session begins." I cast a sideways glance at Christine, whose eyes were trained on Molly, a look of consternation on her face.

Andy grinned and said out of the corner of his mouth, "Don't mind her. She's a perfectionist, that's all, but if you follow her advice, Molly here will be the most well-behaved dog on your block."

"And *I* certainly hope *you're* right about that."

I bade the friendly Andy a warm goodbye and prepared to drag Molly back to the parking lot before I was forced to endure another encounter with Christine. Halfway across the lawn, I passed a tall, dark-haired man walking in Christine's direction. He wore a light blue button-down shirt that had the name of the recycling center stitched into the breast and a pair of khaki pants with a razor-edged crease down the front.

Putting two and two together, I reversed directions and approached Christine with the brightest smile I could manage.

This time, whether it was due to the presence of the man I assumed to be her husband, or if she'd just gotten her ya-yas out by tormenting me throughout the class, Christine's demeanor was less combative. She returned my smile with one that actually reached her eyes.

"Good work, Everly," she said, glancing down at Molly, whose attention was still on Brutus the pug as he and his owner meandered toward the parking lot. "Have you met my husband, Ron?" she gestured to the man in the khakis and confirmed my suspicion.

"No," I replied, "It's nice to meet you."

"Likewise," Ron replied easily, "though you're not quite what I was expecting based on Ernie's description."

Ernie had been talking about me. Great.

My mouth flattened into a line, and I rolled my eyes, "I'm sure whatever he had to say was less than complimentary."

"Quite the contrary, actually," Ron said with a laugh. "I suppose he wasn't so keen on your involvement in his murder investigation, but deep down I'd say my brother-in-law admires your spunk."

83

I bit down a smart retort since Christine was, after all, Ernie's sister. "Yes, well, then I'm guessing he isn't too thrilled that I discovered *another* dead body just the other day."

Christine's eyes widened slightly, and she shook her head in time with her husband. "It's terrible what happened to Spencer," she said, "and now poor Ron has to deal with the fallout." She raised a hand and patted her husband on the back and appeared as though she might elaborate on the subject when the woman with the poodle perm approached and stole her attention away.

That was fine with me since it left me alone with 'poor Ron.'

"From what Ernie said, the accident was a fluke, a random chain of bad luck," I said, stating the obvious and hoping Ron would open up without the necessity of overtly pumping him for information. He seemed like a nice guy on the surface, but if anyone had both means and opportunity to dump that load of paper on Spencer's head, it would be him. What I didn't know was whether he had a motive.

"It sure was," Ron sighed, but didn't elaborate.

"It's just such an odd way for someone to go," I hedged, "especially since the area where Spencer was standing was clearly marked as a danger zone. He couldn't have missed the warning signs."

Ron nodded, his eyes taking on a faraway look. "I know it was an accident, but I feel partially responsible. I'm the one who cut off the alarm after Spencer complained about the noise. At least one good thing came from all of this. The town has agreed to release emergency funds to replace those old gates with proper roll-down doors. They'll be a lot more secure, and they'll reduce the noise from the alarms so nothing like this can ever happen again."

"Did you know Spencer well? Did he complain a lot? How often does the shredder run unattended?"

That might have been too many questions in a row, but Ron answered anyway.

"Not more than to say hello if we met on the street, and no, he didn't complain a lot. But he did have some pull with the town, so the word came down that we had to do something about the noise. Night runs only happened once a month at most. That's why we didn't hire on for a night shift. Most of the paper deliveries come in during the day. I think this was the first Saturday run ever."

"So no one could have anticipated the paper would fall when it did."

Ron looked at me funny. "No. You don't think it was an accident?"

"What? No, I didn't say that." I was beginning to wonder if Spencer was wrong about it being murder. The more I learned, the more it looked like it had to be an accident. "I was just thinking about how he probably didn't see it coming, and at least it was a quick death."

I'm pretty sure that point of view creeped Ron out because he gave me the brush off and joined his wife, leaving me with more questions than answers.

CHAPTER 13

One minute, I was sound asleep, the next, I was standing in the middle of my bedroom with my hands pressed over my ears. It only took a few seconds to locate the source of the panic-inducing noise.

Until the moment I saw her silhouetted in the window, head back, and her throat swelling with the sound, I wasn't aware a dog could imitate a siren so accurately.

"Molly. What are you doing?" At the sound of my voice, she fell silent enough for me to hear the thin, distant echo of an actual siren carried on the night air. "It's two o'clock in the morning. Go back to sleep." Which was exactly what I intended to do once my adrenaline level dropped, and my heart settled back to a normal rhythm.

Except, now that she was up, Molly decided she needed to visit her favorite corner of the yard, and judging by the frantic nature of her gotta-pee dance, there was no time to spare.

"Give me a second." I dragged a thin robe over my sleep shorts and tee and stepped out onto the back porch.

The full moon's light was bright enough to lay long shadows over the dewdrop diamonds littering the lawn. A sight lovely enough to nearly make up for the heart-stopping moment of panic that had dragged me outside for a look.

Mine.

Every so often, the pride of ownership bubbled up from some hidden nook of my psyche. All of this was mine. Well, mine and Catherine's. But mostly mine.

"Freaking piece of crap, son of a biscuit." A feminine voice touched by the music of the south floated over the fence.

My across-the-street neighbor, Neena. No one had seen her since the day we laid her husband to rest, and his killer attacked me in my own home. Rumor had it, she'd gone back home for a visit.

86

What was she doing outside at this hour of the night? I had to know.

Bare feet made little noise on the wet grass, and since David had oiled my garden gate, it was also silent. That's why, while it was not my intention, I managed to sneak up on Neena, whose back was to me while she struggled with one of those manual push mowers, the type that looked like a set of wheels with blades twining between.

"What are you doing?"

She jumped about a foot and rounded on me. Not all the shadows on her face came from the slanting light of the moon. Hair uncombed, wearing a ratty tee and baggy shorts, it didn't look like Neena had been putting personal hygiene at the top of her daily to-do list.

I felt bad, but I still wanted to know what she was doing.

"Grief, Everly. You about scared the life out of me. Why are you sneaking around in the middle of the night?"

"Why are you trying to mow your lawn in the middle of the night?" I countered. "And if you're still in town, why haven't you been answering your door? Have you been hiding inside all these weeks?"

Neena turned away, but not before the moonlight picked out the single tear sliding down her cheek.

"Why would you care? That madman almost killed you, and all because of Hudson. I can't imagine how you'd ever want to speak to me again."

What kind of people must Neena have come from if she thought I'd blame her for a set of events over which she had no control?

Stepping closer, I laid a hand on her arm, gave it a consoling squeeze. "The attack wasn't your fault. Or Hudson's, either, and look, I'm fine. I've been worried about you, though. We thought you'd gone back home. Has the old witch been a problem?" Hudson's mother wasn't one of my favorite people.

Neena's shoulders rounded. "Not since the day after the funeral when she called to tell me I was dead to her, and that everyone would hate me because she'd lost her precious son, and if I possessed even an ounce of decency, I would go to the courthouse and take back my maiden name."

87

"Viola Montayne is a boil on the butt of humanity. You should ignore everything she said." My heart breaking for her, I put my arms around Neena and gave her the hug I knew she needed. "Everything, do you hear me? It's all going to be okay. I'm here for you, and so is Jacy."

Neena hugged me back, and I felt most of the tension leave her body. No one should have to carry the weight of such loss alone, and I wished I'd tried harder to make sure she was okay.

"Now, put that contraption back in the garage. You will not be sneaking around at night trying to stay out of sight. In fact, I'll throw you a freaking parade if you want. Just to show the evil spawn that she's not the boss of you. There'd be floats, and banners, and even a marching band."

"Maybe we can table that idea for the time bein'. It wouldn't be seemly." Still, the mental image pulled a smile out of her.

"I will as long as you promise not to hide out in the house anymore." Wide awake now, I asked, "Would you like to see something I think you'll find interesting? Or is it too weird to go visiting in the middle of the night?"

"I haven't seen or spoken to another livin' soul that wasn't a cashier at the all-night grocery store for so long I'm starved for conversation. If you're up for company, count me in."

We detoured through the back yard to retrieve Molly and went inside. There wasn't a thing I could think of to say that would prepare her for Catherine's hidden space, so I didn't even try. The daybreak-bright moonlight couldn't penetrate the blinds I'd not bothered to raise, so the addition sat in nearly total darkness until I flipped on the light switches one by one.

" Oh, my goodness." Neena's hand came up to cover her heart at the sight of the mannequin bodies. She blinked and stared. "I can't ... I don't ... this is—"

"The term you are searching for is *hot mess with an artistic flair.*"

Neena flashed me a look, then motioned toward the mannequins. "Those lights are downright genius. See how these two go together? In the first, she thinned the plastic over the belly so the lights would create a glow, and then she brought the floral motif up from the groin area to bloom over the breasts. It's the hope of motherhood. So simple, yet so powerful."

88

I wasn't usually so dense when it came to subtext in art, but I'd totally missed that one.

"I see it now. And the second one, with those slashes of black and," I looked closer, "I think those are spokes from a bicycle wheel sticking out. That one is symbolic of a barren womb." How Catherine must have suffered.

"The best art happens when the artist can give form to the triumph and sorrow of the soul."

Ignoring the clutter, Neena scanned the space for more. "I never knew. Two years we were neighbors, and I had no idea."

"If it's any consolation, I don't think anyone did. At least no one local, because, as I'm sure you've learned, this is a small town and it runs on gossip. There's no way people knew all this was here and didn't pass along an opinion about it. None."

"Do you mind? Or is it too late? I can come back another time, but I'm dyin' to see the rest."

"Not at all. I'm wide awake and interested to get your take on the artwork. You've already given me new insight on the torsos." There were more original pieces than I'd not noticed on my first time through or even my second. It was like Disneyland— impossible to process in one visit.

Neena was starting up the stairs ahead of me when I remembered the subject matter on the painting on the easel. If seeing such naked sorrow over the death of a husband could make me cry, surely Neena's reaction would be even stronger given her similar circumstances.

"Sorry." I shoved past her and thundered ahead just in time to trip over the top step and go down in a face plant that was probably a level ten on the scale of clumsy.

"What was that all about? Are you all right?"

I rolled over and took stock. "Skinned my knee, but otherwise, I think I'll survive." I took the hand Neena offered and let her help me up from the floor. As soon as I was on my feet, her gaze moved past me to take in the loft and fell on the painting.

Neena sucked in a breath and held it for a long beat. "The angel is her husband."

"Yes. His photo was on the wall downstairs when I moved in."

Another beat passed before Neena spoke again. "You know, I'm not sure which makes me the saddest. This painting, or that she kept all her talent locked up in a room where no one could see."

It took iron control to keep from pointing out we were here in the middle of the night because she'd been locked in her house for weeks, and I didn't have to anyway, because she beat me to the punch.

"You know what? He might have been her angel, but I think you're mine."

By then, it was closer to three in the morning, and my brain wasn't as clear as it had been before, so I frowned.

"This," she said, waving a hand to indicate the entire add-on space, "has been me. Locked away where no one could see the best, most interesting parts of me. The scary thing is that hiding out started to feel normal." My bones creaked she hugged me so hard. "Do you know what I'm going to do? I'm going to go home and go to bed, and I'm going to get up tomorrow while the sun is shining, and I'm going to go to the grocery store. I'm going to mow my lawn in the daylight, and if you don't mind, I'm going to come back here and look at this painting again."

"The offer for a parade still stands."

Neena gave me a genuine smile. "I think I'll pass on that, but I won't be backing down if Viola Montayne makes another one of her nasty comments. How that woman ever raised a man like Hudson, I'll never know."

In another minute, I stood alone in front of the painting, listening to the sound of Neena's retreat.

CHAPTER 14

The three of us stood just inside the doorway of Catherine's lair and contemplated the sheer volume of items crammed into the space.

"Kinda feels like I'm standing at the foot of Everest looking up and wondering if I'll survive the climb," Neena said.

"We could just close the door and forget I ever found that key. That wouldn't be the worst thing, right?"

Jacy gave my arm a less-than-gentle pinch. "You know I love you more than shoes, but you're killing me here. All I've ever wanted to do is open up a little vintage shop. Not your average second-hand store, but more of a curated collection. Plus some local arts and crafts. Stuff that appeals to the tourists. You've got everything right here to do what I've always wanted to do, and you're acting like it's some kind of cross to bear."

Rubbing my arm, I turned to her in surprise. "I've known you since we were both in diapers and you've never said a word about this before. Why is that?"

She flushed. "Come on, you know I'm never going to have the money to open a shop. The startup costs are ridiculous. First and last on a rental space, insurance, and store fixtures alone would eat up my entire savings account, and then what? I'd stand in my empty space and sell air to tourists? It's a pipe dream for me, but you have plenty of room right here, and the stock ready-made."

It showed in her tone that Jacy didn't begrudge me falling into a situation that she'd only dreamed about, and that was just more of her inherent Jacy-ness.

"You could have said something. Now I feel like a lousy, insensitive friend."

"What would be the point? It's not your dream, and why should it be? But this is never going to happen for me."

I'd almost forgotten about Neena when her voice boomed. "Why the hell not?"

Exasperated, Jacy huffed. "Because of all the things I just said. The startup costs and the stock and just when would I have time to run a shop? Because I couldn't quit my job on a whim. I've got a baby on the way who, I'm pretty sure, is going to need a few things."

"I heard you the first time," Neena grinned. "And I want in on it."

"In on what? My fantasy store? Sure, have a ball." Jacy waggled her fingers. "Poof, you're involved."

Neena's pointed finger circled the room. "There's your stock. You'll take it on consignment, so no money out of pocket there." She looked to me for confirmation, and I nodded. "You might not know this about me, but I have a nose for finding bargains. I bet I could rustle up shelving and racks for next to nothing."

Getting into the spirit, I pointed out, "I know where there's a prime location about to become vacant, and I do have some experience with generating attention for an event. I don't see why I couldn't do the same for your shop."

Unable to accept that her dream could become a reality, Jacy shook her head. "Even with all of that, I'd have to sell my soul for enough money to open the doors, and if it failed, then what? I can't take a chance like that when I'm just getting ready to start a family."

But now that Neena had the bit firmly between her teeth, she was raring to go.

"Look, I'll admit to knowing diddly squat about running a shop, but I've always wanted my own little art gallery, and I need to do something with the money from Hudson's life insurance. What do you say we get together and make both of our dreams come true? You wanna be partners?" Neena stuck out a hand and waited patiently for Jacy to decide.

Jacy bit her lip, and I could see she wanted to jump in but wasn't convinced, so I stepped in and bought her a little time. "There's no need to rush into anything, but I don't see how it could hurt to do some research and put together a list of costs. Once you have solid numbers in front of you, it will be easier to make a decision."

"Okay," and on that Jacy and Neena came to an agreement.

"Since you're going to want dibs on all of this stuff, we don't have to start sorting through it now." I was all for heading back toward the door.

"How can we consider using your stuff as the basis for our stock if we don't get a good look at the merchandise?" Neena countered. "Besides, you still need to pick out some pieces for the yard-sale charity table."

I'd told them about being cornered by the church ladies. "Maybe I should give them the torso lights. Can you imagine the look on Martha Tipton's face if I came rolling up in old Sally and pulled one of those out of the back seat?"

I wouldn't do any such thing, but only because Catherine had kept her artwork hidden away from her neighbors. I might never know her reasons, but I'd never betray her memory.

"I won't do it, though. They're starting to grow on me."

"Too bad they don't give off more light." Jacy's muffled voice drifted from some dark corner. "Come help me move a few of these crates out of the way so I can get to the window."

"What crates? Where are you?"

"Behind the wall of dressers. There's a whole maze back here."

With Neena following, I headed toward the piled up dressers, but couldn't see a way to get behind them.

"How did you get in there? I can't see an opening."

"If you crawl under those three tables on the right, it's kind of like a tunnel."

The look I exchanged with Neena held an entire conversation in its silence. She was the one to ask the obvious question. "What leap of logic made you think to crawl under those tables?"

"I was thinking I'd find a way to get to the windows, and I did. Now get in here and help me move some of this stuff."

At least the floors were moderately clean. "This is ridiculous. Are you sure there's room for all of us back there?" I'd have sworn the dressers were up against the wall, which proved my depth perception wasn't what it should be.

I checked with Neena. "You're not claustrophobic, are you?"

"Only one way to find out." She went first. "There's never a dull moment with the two of you, is there?"

93

Since the question seemed rhetorical, I declined to answer and concentrated on watching her the soles of her feel moving ahead of me through the thin shafts of light that occasionally filtered through the spaces between the tables.

My knees were beginning to protest just as the makeshift tunnel ended and I popped up into a narrow corridor between the backs of the dressers and a bunch of old wooden milk crates stacked above eye level along the outer wall.

"What's in them? Did you look?" Having found a closet full of mannequin heads in the main house, I wouldn't hazard a guess at the contents.

"Dunno. I gave that one a nudge, and it didn't seem too heavy, but I didn't want to chance it." The top box was stacked over petite Jacy's head.

"Move aside, I'm the tallest." Neena curled her fingers over the edge of the top box in front of the nearest window and gave it a yank. Glass rattled against glass.

In the dim light, we stared at the contents. "That was anti-climactic," Neena said. "It's nothing but a bunch of old milk bottles."

Milk crates, milk bottles. I guess we should have seen that one coming. She pulled down another to join the first then reached up and fiddled with the top of the roller blind. I heard a slither and a thump as it fell toward the sill, and then I blinked in the sudden brightness.

Going down the line, Jacy jiggled a few of the boxes and listened for the tinkling of glass. "You know," she said, "I've seen milk bottles like this selling for ten bucks or so in antique shops, and the crates can be worth a lot more."

"Enough to make a worthy donation to the charity table? I'm pretty sure I could part with two or three and not miss them at all."

"You just don't want to be bothered with sorting through all this stuff, so you're jumping on the first thing that comes to hand," Jacy pouted. "Why don't you set one aside and we'll explore some more just in case we find something better."

I sighed. "Sorry, I've been struggling with feeling like I'm prying, and you're right, I am looking at this all wrong. I need to think of it as an adventure, not as a chore."

"That's the spirit," Neena said as she pulled down the top box in front of the second window. "I only talked to Catherine a few times. She wasn't exactly a recluse, but she didn't get out much during her last years. Thinking back, I'm sorry I didn't take the time to visit her more often, but what I knew of her, she had a kind soul."

"So everyone says," I admitted.

"Well, she didn't strike me as the kind to have a vengeful spirit, so if you're worried about her coming back to haunt you, I think you're safe." Neena was joking.

"No, Catherine's spirit isn't the one that worries me." I was not.

In the end, each of us shoved a milk crate ahead of us and crawled back out the way we had gone in.

Neena lifted her hair up to let air circulate across the back of her neck. "That was a workout. I feel like I've been dipped in bacon fat and rolled in flour."

Even *daisy fresh under any circumstances* Jacy was looking a little flushed with the heat. "I say we give this another hour and then drive up to camp for a nice dip in the lake."

"You're on."

At the end of the hour, Jacy threw up her hands in defeat. "Okay, I'm not too big to admit when I'm wrong. This is a hot mess, and I can see why you've been dreading doing it. We're just moving boxes from one pile to another. The only way to tackle a job this size is with a keep/sell/discard system. You need to be ruthless, and you need to clear an area to hold each set of items."

"That's a good idea as long as the sell items end up in our shop." Neena had no intention of letting go of the idea once it was on the table.

I diffused the situation by dragging them out of the back rooms and up to the lake. Molly took to the water like she'd been born to swim, and Spencer, if he bothered to check in, had the good sense to keep quiet.

Back home that evening, I put a frozen pizza in the oven—I still hadn't worked up the courage to order in—and grabbed a shower. Standing in the doorway, toweling off my hair, I faced the drop-top desk that was still filled with Catherine's personal papers.

"You know what, Molly. It's time to be ruthless." The pizza needed a few minutes more, so I went to the garage for a box. I threw out Christmas cards, letters from friends, and bills. I ate my pizza while methodically emptying cubbyholes and didn't stop until I got down to the drawers.

The first one I opened was full of envelopes in every size and color. I kept a handful. The rest, enough to half fill a plastic shopping bag, I set aside to go in the yard sale because it seemed a shame to throw them away. The next drawer held a surprise. Catherine had kept a diary—or to be more precise, a bunch of them.

I pulled out the one on top and read the latest passage, written in a spidery hand, and dated just before Catherine went to the nursing home.

It is with great joy that I write today. Very soon now, I shall be shed of this mortal coil. How I long to be reunited with my dearest Basil. A week, maybe two, the doctor said in such solemn tones. How could he know that he filled my heart with joy?

The arrangements are made, the checks written. Tomorrow, I shall leave my home to die in a strange bed. So long I have been alone in the world, there are none left of my blood to hold my hand or shed a tear as I go into that good night. But I am not afraid. My faith will carry me through until I rest in the arms of the angel who will comfort me and bear me home.

Overcome, I sat on down on the edge of the bed and didn't order Molly down when she slithered up beside me and swiped her tongue over my tear-drenched cheek. I wasn't sure if I could read more, but I knew I couldn't stop.

The lovely young Judith came from Hospice today to ensure my affairs were in order, and I lied right to her face. The truth is, I had always planned to die alone, in my own bed, and so I have held on to this house long past the time when I should have let it go.

It's a good house, though I fancy it has grown tired of the likes of me. I did not tell Judith that I have made no provision for its disposal, nor have I made out a will. The efficient Judith would not approve of my whimsy, but I much prefer for the hand of fate to choose if or when this house gets passed on. I only hope the next owner will find joy and love in equal measure, and that there will someday be the sound of children's laughter where none has been.

Today, I will sit at my desk and listen to the echoes of my memories. I will say goodbye to this home, to this life, and prepare myself gladly to take on the next one.

I'm ready now. Goodbye.

When I finished, I sat for a moment to get my bearings, then put the diary back where I had found it and closed the drawer. Later, I promised myself, I would get to know this woman through the words that she had written.

CHAPTER 15

On the day of the yard sale committee meeting, my phone rang shortly after Molly and I returned from our morning constitutional. I'd settled down on the deck with a cup of coffee to watch her put the final touches on ruining my lilies.

"Is this Everly Dupree?" I didn't recognize the number on the screen or the caller's voice.

"It is."

"My name is Kendra Charles. You worked for my brother, Spencer. His landlord gave me your number."

The infamous sister. "I'm sorry for your loss. Is there anything I can do to help?"

"Could you possibly find the time to meet me with the keys so I can get into his office? I'd like to clear everything out as soon as possible."

"Tell her I'm sorry." Spencer popped up a little too close, and I had to take a hasty step back. "And tell her I love her."

"Of course—"

"Tell her."

I glared at Spencer and made a split-second decision. "I can be there at ten."

"Tell her I acted like an ass, and I didn't mean any of the things I said."

The air cooled until my breath turned into puffs of steam.

"Thank you, I'll see you then." She hung up.

Annoyed, I faced my unwanted guest. "Cut the theatrics, Spencer. I told you the rules right from the beginning. You stay out of my private spaces, you don't come around when I'm with other people, and I don't give messages to family from beyond the grave. You're two for three already, and I'm at the end of my limit."

Listen, I was happy to help find his killer. Happy isn't the right word, so let's just say I was willing to help find his killer, but people talk. You tell one person you can see their lost loved one and pass along a final message, and the next thing you know, half your neighbors are looking at you funny. The other half are lining up at your door to see if you can channel their dead relatives. No. Nope. Not happening.

Even if I wanted to pass messages between the living and the dead, I couldn't. This wasn't some skill I had developed, or an innate ability to see beyond the veil. I'd have known long before now if I had some uncanny psychic talent. This was a haunting, pure and simple. Beyond my control according to Internet sources I'd managed to track down on the subject. Then again, none of the suggestions I'd found had helped ghost-proof my home, so I didn't put much stock in the information found on websites.

My coffee froze solid.

Launching out of my chair, I crossed my arms and glared at Spencer. He mimicked my pose and glared back.

"You're a jerk." I had an urge to throw my coffee cup at him, not that it would do any good. Instead, I marched into the kitchen and put it in the microwave to reheat. "You know that?"

As soon as I pulled the cup out, the coffee froze again. You can mess with a lot of things in my life, but not my first cup of the day.

"Keep it up, and you're on your own. I don't have to help you at all. Not really."

The air changed, and not just the temperature this time, but the weight of it in my lungs. It felt heavy and moist, almost pregnant with the force of Spencer's anger.

A series of thumping sounds in the living room drew me in that direction. I had to squeeze past Molly to get there. I'd let go of her leash, and now she was doing the series of circles she always did when Spencer showed up—three to the left, three to the right. Only this time, when she finished, she repeated the pattern.

I stepped into the room to see books flying off my shelves to land in piles on the floor.

"Real mature, Spencer. Have a temper tantrum, why don't you?"

"Do what I want, and I'll stop." Maybe it was the way his energy weighted the air or maybe it was just the force of his emotion, but his voice echoed menacingly.

"Trash the house. I don't care. Just remember, this is Molly's home, too." Fury carried me to the hall table, where I grabbed my purse and stalked out the door. As expected, Spencer followed. He followed me to the garage, got in the car, and continued to harangue me all the way to the office, but he couldn't follow me inside. I'll admit I felt pretty good about slamming the door in his face.

I should have washed my hands of him, but I'd made a promise to help, and I keep my promises. If his sister intended to clean out the office, I'd need to back up his computer files to my cloud account before she arrived. There might be information on there that I'd need later.

By the time I got the system booted, I only had ten minutes of my hour left, and the backup would take fifteen.

Naturally, Kendra arrived early and looked so much like her brother when he was annoyed, I wondered if they were twins.

"I'm Everly. We spoke on the phone." I offered my hand and noticed hers felt cold. "I have a meeting in a little while, but I'd be happy to help you pack until I have to leave."

"No need, the movers will be here any minute. The faster this is done, the sooner I can put it all behind me."

I searched for some vestige of emotion in her face. Just enough to tempt me into breaking my rule to give her Spencer's message if I could find a way without sounding too intrusive.

While I thought it over, Kendra poked her head into the supply closet, then into my former office. She was just heading toward his when the computer beeped, signaling the backup was complete. I could walk away now and not attempt to make a fool of myself.

Instead, I picked up the photo of Spencer and Molly from his desk and handed it to Kendra. "Spencer didn't talk about his family much."

She looked at it for a moment, then her face hardened, and she dropped the photo into the trash can. "No reason why he should. Family is a word for the people foisted off on you by genetics. Nothing more."

If she really believed that, I felt sorry for Kendra. My impression was that she wouldn't have been receptive to Spencer's apology itself, and certainly not to me even if I could figure out a way to relay it. Her next statement proved my point.

"Now, If you don't mind, I need to finish cleaning up my brother's final mess so I can get back to my life."

"Whatever happened between you and your brother, I think he cared for you." It wasn't exactly what he wanted me to say.

"Well, Merry Sunshine, you clearly didn't know him very well."

Brushing past, Kendra left me awkwardly standing there while she went out to greet and direct the movers who had arrived.

"Just the file cabinet and the computers in the truck. Everything else goes out on the curb. I presume this burg has some sort of garbage pickup." She poked her head back in to dismiss me. "Come back in an hour to lock up. We'll be gone by then."

"If it's all the same to you, we're having a town-wide yard sale soon. I could arrange for someone to come in and clear the office of whatever you don't plan to take if you're willing to consider the contents as a donation."

"Done." She turned to the movers. "You heard the woman. Computers and file cabinets." Fifteen minutes later, she was gone.

The second I slid behind the wheel of my car, Spencer got in my face. "Did you tell her?"

"No. I didn't. I'm sorry, but she wasn't interested in anything I had to say on the subject."

"You didn't try hard enough."

"Maybe not. Or maybe you should have tried harder while you were living." A chill began to steal through the car. "Don't do it, Spencer. Why don't you go haunt someone else?"

He didn't, but he also didn't follow me into the yard sale committee meeting, or maybe he couldn't, a fact for which I was grateful.

Martha Tipton, her eyes alight with happiness, practically pounced on me when I walked through the door. Converted from a former schoolhouse, the town office still smelled faintly of chalk dust and children.

"You're here."

"I'm sorry, I know I'm late."

"Come right in, and don't worry about a thing." She threaded her arm through mine and took a grip on my bicep to keep me from

101

rabbiting, I supposed. "We only have a few minutes to finish up the planning before the reporter from the Northern Observer arrives."

"A reporter is coming?"

"Why, yes. I got to thinking after you agreed to join us, that with your planning skills, we could build ... what's it called ... hum around the event."

"I think you mean buzz."

"That's it. Right in here." I saw the rest of her cronies through wire mesh encased with safety glass. Bess and Patricia sat on old classroom chairs meant for smaller behinds, and neither of them looked happy.

"Did she tell you what she's done?" Bess looked like she'd been sucking on a lemon. "I hope you have some contacts in the circus world because that's what this has turned into. Three rings with Martha in the center on her trick pony."

"Did you just call Everly a one-trick pony?" Patricia came to my defense.

"What? No, you old—"

In the interest of stopping the bickering, I interrupted. "Ladies. Please. What have you planned so far?"

Bess glared daggers at Martha. "Well, that's just the thing, isn't it? This one went and took out a full-page spread in the Observer without waiting for us to get together."

"Well, I had to, didn't I? The deadline for submissions was yesterday, and I didn't want to miss it."

"You didn't have to go overboard," Patricia chided and then explained. "She embellished."

"Only a little." Martha turned to me. "I know all about those parties you've put together. Your mother bragged you up. All I said was that we would offer a petting zoo with pony rides for the kids, and refreshments."

Bess's voice rose to a screeching pitch. "Refreshments? That's putting a coat of whitewash on a prune. You said food trucks. Plural. Do you know anyone with a food truck? Do you, Martha Tipton? If you do, I'll dance a jig in the town square."

"I'd pay good money to see that," Patricia muttered, and then bit her lip to keep from saying more, but the twinkle in her eye was enough for me.

If Bess heard the comment, she chose to ignore Patricia. "And a petting zoo. Honestly, Are you keeping small barnyard animals and ponies hidden up your backside?"

That mental image was enough to give me nightmares for a week, and it made Patricia snort out loud.

"Ladies," I caught their attention and channeled my mother's sternest manner. "That's enough." Bess tried to flay the skin from my bones with a look, and when all she got from me was a raised eyebrow over direct eye contact, she twisted in her seat and turned her head away.

"Is that all, Martha?"

"No," she almost mumbled, "There's more."

Why did I think the more was going to be worse? Because Martha couldn't look me in the eye. "I might have said the pony rides and petting zoo would be free." She sounded miserable. "I thought it would draw in more families if there were something fun for kids to do."

At this point, Bess wasn't speaking to anyone, and Martha looked ready to cry, so Patricia jumped in and explained. "When Hackinaw got all that grant money, the first thing they did was petition the state to put a two-lane stretch of road to cut down on travel time from the Thruway to the northern woods. Now, instead of running through Mooselick River, half the tourist traffic bypasses us at sixty-five miles an hour."

"The diner and the motel seem to do okay."

"For now because they're picking up the overflow because the rest of the hotels haven't gone up. Give it another two years, and we're going to be living in a ghost town. We thought if we could turn Mooselick River into a destination for at least one weekend a year, it would be a start on boosting business."

"So you three cooked up this scheme, and then Martha got excited, and now we need to come through with food trucks, a petting zoo, and free pony rides."

"In about an hour before that reporter shows up and makes us eat crow." Bess still had her nose in the air.

"Okay." I pulled out my phone. "I can work with that."

I spent the next half hour daisy chaining my way through my contacts list until my favorite caterer gave me the number of a friend with a brand new license to sell pulled pork and chicken out of the back of a converted Winnebago. Pulled pork guy said he could scare up a few more trucks as long as I could get the owners a little free publicity. I agreed to blast out names on social media and to make sure the reporter talked up the food offerings in the upcoming article. He agreed to make the calls right away, and email me the contact information and descriptions for whoever he could line up.

He also put me in touch with a young married couple who mainly raised sheep and alpacas, but maintained a small petting zoo at their farm which they opened up to grade school tours in the spring. They were happy to bring their animals to town. All I had to do was help arrange transport and hire a professional photographer to shoot some stills for their website. That was an easy one, and I called in a favor to make it happen.

"That was amazing." Martha almost bounced in her chair.

"Doesn't let you off the hook," Bess said. "We're still missing the pony rides." I got the feeling she was hoping I'd fail.

"Oh, I saved that for last since it was the easiest." Worst one, first one—my Grammie Dupree had drilled that piece of wisdom into me when I was young.

I picked up the phone and tapped out a set of numbers I knew by heart. Dani Painter didn't owe me any favors. If anything, it was the other way around, but if her schedule were clear, we'd have our free pony rides. I had other reasons for wanting to talk to Dani, but Bess didn't need to know my personal business.

"Hey, Ev. I just heard a rumor that you and Paul split up. Are you okay?"

"I'm fine." And I meant it, which was kind of a big deal. "I moved back home, and I'm doing just great. How are things at the ranch?" Given that the Hastings counted among the ranch's top-tier of donors if they were having legal problems bad enough to put the funding in jeopardy, Dani would have more info than Patrea.

That she answered cheerfully set my mind slightly more at ease. "Fantastic as always. I'm blessed."

I explained what I need from her, and after checking the dates, she enthusiastically agreed. "You'll give me the standard rate for the day?"

"Of course." We chatted for a few moments more, and when I hung up, Bess huffed. "Standard rate? That'll probably cost the town a pretty penny."

"Dani runs Hope Ranch. They're a not-for-profit facility with two specific goals. To rescue horses and to train those horses to work in the therapy center. She does incredible work, and her standard rate won't cost you a thing. I'd have happily spent the day volunteering there whether she brought the ponies or not. If you have a problem with her using the day as a rehabilitation exercise, then let me know now, and I'll call her back."

"I've heard of Hope Ranch," Patricia put Bess to shame. "They help at-risk youth, veterans, people struggling with addiction."

"That's exactly right. She's a firm believer that giving to others is one of the best things a person can do to grow and find inner strength. That's why I knew she'd come if she had an opening. If you get a chance on the day, you should watch how handling the ponies and giving delight to children is a healing experience."

"Would she mind more than one volunteer?" Patricia asked. "I know I'm not as spry as I once was, but I've always had a way with horses, and I'd love to pitch in."

"I know Dani would be delighted to have you. There's always room for someone with enough generosity of spirit to want to help." It was a dig at Bess, who had the sense to keep her mouth shut until the reporter showed up.

At that point, she took over and made it seem as if she had been the one to arrange everything. Martha looked fit to kill, and Patricia's eyes rolled so many times I worried she'd give herself a headache. Once I got the email from the ringleader of the food truck brigade, I passed the details along and tried to bow out, but not before the reporter figured out who I was.

I spent ten more minutes dodging questions that had nothing to do with the yard sale and everything to do with my imploding marriage. Finally, citing a prior engagement, I made my escape before he could pry any deeper.

CHAPTER 16

Still fuming, I pulled in at the grocery store on my way home. In the pet food section, I had just wrestled an industrial-sized bag of dog food into my cart when I heard a sniff behind me and turned to see Christine Murray staring at the bag like it had essence of skunk written in big letters across the front.

"Is that what you're feeding Molly?"

No, you idiot, I eat beef-flavored pellets for breakfast.

"She likes this brand. Why? Is there a problem?"

"Did you even read the label? She's a purebred; she should be eating organic and grain-free." Circling me, Christine plucked the offending food out of my cart and put it back on the shelf. "This one." She selected another bag that cost the same but was about a third the size. "It's made from grass-fed beef and poultry, and has no by-products or grain in it."

"She'll polish that off in two days." I'd go broke feeding her at this rate.

"It's more nutritious, so she'll eat less of it."

Somehow I doubted that. I'd seen Molly dig up a grub and scarf it down. She wasn't that picky of an eater, and the brand I'd chosen was nationally known. It wasn't like I'd gone with something generic.

After that, I swear she'd decided to wait me out and make sure I left with her choice because, at every turn of the aisle, there was Christine checking my cart. I finally gave in and hit the checkout where I got the shock of the day.

"Hey, Robin. I didn't realize you were working here now."

Snapping her gum, Robin scanned a package of Romaine lettuce twice, put it in the bag, then peering at the readout, pulled it back out and scanned it two more times. To her credit, I think on the second pass she was trying to rectify the mistake. "It's my second day."

The scanner dinged three more times, and I watched the total for the lettuce rise to more than twenty dollars before she shrugged and rang up the rest of my purchases. Two people behind me decided to change lanes. Wise of them. I'd be more careful in the future.

After paying my bill, I waited by the customer service desk to have someone with more than half a brain give me a refund on the lettuce. Based on the resignation with which the transaction was processed, I didn't think Robin had a bright future as a grocery store cashier.

On my way out, just inside the sliding doors, I noticed someone had put up a community bulletin board—mostly because one of the handwritten flyers stopped me dead.

Jeep for Sale. I read. *Excellent condition. Too many upgrades to list. All reasonable offers considered.*

The slash and slant of the penmanship looked familiar. If I weren't mistaken, the phone number on the fluttering tabs would lead me to the person who'd written the poison pen letter to Spencer, and I didn't even need to tear one off. It was a number I already knew.

Molly's subdued greeting when I walked through the door should have warned me something was wrong inside, but with my thoughts occupied, I wasn't paying attention. I only noticed something was amiss when, without looking, I dropped my purse on the table in the hallway, and it landed on the floor. I'd been robbed.

"Some watchdog you are," I said to Molly as I bent to retrieve my purse and pull out my phone. I'd dialed the nine and had my finger over the one when she went into her spinning routine.

Spencer.

"We weren't robbed, were we?"

Tail wagging, she turned and trotted down the hall. Keeping my phone in hand just in case, I followed her into the living room where I found the hall table. We had not been robbed. This was worse.

If Spencer weren't already dead, I'd have killed him without a shred of remorse. My living room looked like some bizarre version of Stonehenge. Tables piled halfway to the ceiling, the sofa perched

107

precariously across the top, all the knick-knacks from the shelves balanced along the edges. It was worse than Stonehenge—it was Jenga made from furniture. I rescued the blue-and-white porcelain bell that had been one of my grandmother's favorites before a single swipe from Molly's tail took the whole mess down.

Backing out, I closed the door, and yelled into the seemingly empty space, "Spencer Charles, if you're listening, you have one hour to clean up the mess you made, or I'll take drastic measures."

Because I needed to blow off steam, I walked to the diner where Jacy should be nearing the end of her shift. Only half the jumpy feeling in the pit of my stomach came from missing lunch, the rest from having had a really lousy day. One that wasn't about to get better in the next few minutes.

"Hey, Ev. Want a turkey club? I just need to finish up with these." Jacy brandished the ketchup bottle she was in the middle of refilling. "Then I'll join you."

"Sounds good." I nodded and took my favorite booth.

As good as the sandwich looked, I couldn't eat until I got the weight off my chest.

"Jace, why are you selling the Jeep?"

"We talked about it, and it's not really suitable for the baby. It's time I had a grown-up vehicle. You know, like a minivan or something a mom would drive."

That was the easy question. I wasn't sure how to broach the hard one.

So, I blurted out, "Brian wrote a threatening letter to Spencer. I found it in his desk drawer. Did you know?"

The smile left her face, but Jacy didn't look away. "I know about that. I didn't at the time, but I do now." Her fingers shook when she raised them to press against her temple. "It was when we first decided to start trying for a baby. We figured I'd get pregnant right away, and it looked like it was going to happen. I had two false positives early on, and we were so sure the second one was real, it got us thinking. So, Brian applied for a mortgage, but he'd just changed jobs, and there was a car loan, and I'd only been working here for a few months, so we didn't have good enough credit."

"But the letter was bad, Jace. He said he wanted to kill Spencer."

She pushed her plate away, leaving the sandwich untouched. "I know. He told me. He also told me he and Spencer had a talk afterward and he apologized. They worked things out between them."

So Spencer had said.

"I don't want you to think less of Brian; he's not that kind of person. Honestly, he's never spoken a harsh word to me no matter what foolish thing I did."

"That's why I was so shocked when I figured it out. I saw the writing on the ad for the Jeep, and then I knew. It seemed completely out of character." I reached across the table to give her hand a squeeze. "But I worked for Spencer long enough to know that the process is not easy, and he wasn't super good with the people-skills part."

Some of the color back in her face, Jacy pulled her plate back and picked up her sandwich. "No, you're right about the process being brutal, but that's no excuse for what Brian wrote. We struggled through three months of providing paperwork and writing insane letters ... like, we had to write a letter to say Brian had the right to access his own bank account because my name happened to come first. That's just ridiculous."

I agreed and told her that wasn't even the worst one I'd seen.

"The same day we got the results on the second false positive, we walked out of the doctor's office in about the worst place you could be, and that was when Spencer called to tell Brian he couldn't get us a mortgage. Brian didn't say a word to me at the time. He went home and took out his frustration by writing that letter. He didn't mean to actually send it, but he did put it in an envelope and address it. By then, we'd sent a few, and not all of them could be submitted by email, so when I found it, I just stuck a stamp on it and dropped it in the mailbox. So you see, it was my fault, really."

There went my suspect, but for once, I was glad to be back at square one. Enough that my appetite returned.

Then Jacy killed it again by squirting ketchup on the pickle spear that garnished her plate and biting off a big chunk. "Spencer might be lousy with his people skills, but he did help us, you know."

"How so?"

"Oh, he had Brian come into his office one day not too long after and laid us out a plan for saving up a down payment while getting our credit into tip-top shape. We took the classes to qualify for a first-time buyer's loan, and it's all working just like he said. We'll be able to go into the bank ourselves in another month, and this time, we'll be approved.

By the time I left the diner, my opinion of Spencer had undergone a subtle shift. Under all the arrogance, there had been a man who loved his dog and helped someone who hadn't treated him well. He had some redeeming qualities that made me feel more receptive to him ... right up until I got home and all the warm fuzzies went out the window.

Spencer had gone into my dresser drawers, pulled out every bra I owned, and hung them off the ceiling fan in my bedroom, where they gently whirled on the slowest speed setting.

"I am done. Do you hear me? Done."

Some habits never fade. Like I had when I was younger, I walked into Leandra Wade's house without knocking. I'd spent so much time there over the years, it felt like home.

Momma Wade would be in her garden at this time of day. The hours between noon and three were what she called the magic hours when the mosquitoes and other biting bugs stuck to shadier areas. I found her, as expected, on her hands and knees, wearing overalls, using a garden fork to scratch compost into the soil. The plants thrived under her green-thumbed care.

She turned when she heard the sliding doors open, and despite everything that had driven me to her door, I had to return her welcoming smile. If for no other reason than that it beamed out at me from beneath the brim of a straw sombrero hand-painted a vibrant purple and decorated with yellow stars.

"You look like a garden wizard." My comment delighted her, and she rose to offer me the kind of hug that made me feel safe. That, too, was one of her gifts.

"I'd ask you what brings you to my humble beds, but I can see your aura vibrating from a mile away. You need spiritual guidance."

"What I need is for you to tell me what you did to me the other day at the lake. There's been an unfortunate side effect, and I need you to get out your sage and clean up your mess." As much as I hated the smell of the burning leaves, I was ready to douse myself in a cloud of the foul smoke if it got rid of the ghost who refused to leave me alone.

"Oh, so now I'm a side effect? You said you would help me."
The air chilled a degree or two. "You promised."

For all of Leandra's talk of spirit guides and energy vortexes
and whatnot, she didn't notice the change in temperature or seem to
see or hear Spencer when he continued to berate me from mere
inches away. I glared at him and then felt like a supreme jerk when
Momma Wade flinched.

"I'm sorry. I'm under a lot of stress right now. You see—"

Her hand went up, and her eyes unfocused for a moment while
she conferred with her guides. It was a look I'd seen more times
than I could count. It was also a look I'd considered an affectation.
Just Momma Wade getting her hoodoo on. My opinion on that had
changed.

"I—" I began to speak.

"Shush now."

Never, in the twenty or so years I'd known her, had Leandra
spoken to me so harshly. I shushed out of pure reflex.

After another minute or two, her eyes popped open. "My
guides inform me that I've done you a great disservice. I used the
wrong blend of oils when I attempted to strengthen your defenses,
and now you've become a conduit."

"A what?"

Her hand went up again. I saw her fingers tremble. "No, not a
conduit and not a channel. Tell it to me in words I understand." The
last she directed to the empty space above and to the right of me and
I'd had enough.

"Crap magnet. Is that the word? Because it doesn't matter
what fancy term your guides use, that's the one that's closest to the
truth. Do you realize I have found two bodies in under a month?
Yeah, that's what happens when you're a crap magnet. And do you
know what's worse? Do you?"

I might have lost my temper in her presence before, but I'd
never, not once, ever directed a rant toward Momma Wade. But I
was on a roll, and there was no stopping me now.

"Thanks to you, I saw Hudson's ghost, and now I'm seeing
Spencer's." Leandra paled. "That's right. He's standing right over
there, and he's pissed off because I didn't try hard enough to mend
his fences for him. I told him I had rules, and not delivering

111

messages to family members is one of them. But did he listen? No, he did not."

I turned to Spencer and kept right on ranting. "You couldn't leave well enough alone, could you? You couldn't follow the rules. No, you had to show up, throw stuff around my house, freeze my coffee, and write things on my mirror. I said I would help you find out what happened to you, and I will, but I don't do messages to family. If you didn't have the guts to be straight with your sister in life, that's a problem for your own conscience. I'm not making it mine."

Whirling back toward her, I pointed at Momma Wade. "You did this to me, you make it stop."

Though I'm not proud of my behavior, the yelling released most of my tension. Now that the storm had passed and sanity had returned, I apologized to Leandra, who asked for my forgiveness and we smoothed everything over.

"Is he still here?" she asked over her shoulder on her way into the house to retrieve her bag of tricks.

He was, and concerned enough about what might happen next to do much more than bluster or he'd have probably flattened a few of her plants. Maybe after a soul goes into the light, all the petty human nonsense falls away. I'd like to think that's true, but Spencer had been an arrogant person in life, and it didn't look to me like death had improved his personality one iota.

"Don't do this! Please, Everly. I'm sorry." He flickered out.

While he was gone, Momma Wade returned. "This won't take long. Are you sure this is what you want?"

"It is."

I closed my eyes against the sage smoke, and only heard Spencer's voice when he returned.

"I cleaned up the house. I won't ever do anything like that again. I promise."

Too little, too late.

Leandra's hands were gentle on my skin as she rubbed oils smelling of herbs and smoke into my skin. She completed each anointing with a kiss, then stepped away.

"Is that it?"

"It is." She launched into some spiel about my third eye, and a shield, and the veil between worlds. I didn't pay that much attention. As far as I was concerned, if the Spencer couldn't bug me again, that was all I needed.

CHAPTER 17

"Come, Molly. Do you want to go for a ride?"

Ride being the magic word, Molly made a beeline for Sally's back seat. I'm sure we made quite the picture driving through town. Me behind the wheel of the red 70s vintage Buick, Molly with her head out the open window.

When we passed the diner, she flicked her tongue in and out of her mouth as she, I assumed, tried to lick the lingering hamburger scent out of the air.

"You need to be on your best behavior, or you won't be invited back." My mother maintained a somewhat neutral stance on dogs. She liked them quite well as long as she didn't have to share her home with one.

As soon as I opened the passenger side door, Molly shot out of the car and onto the porch, where she appeared to remember her manners and sat down obediently on the doormat. It irked to no end that the mere scent of my mother turned Molly into a model of the perfect dog when for me, she tended to forget she even had manners.

"Everly, is that you?" I heard Mom's voice before she opened the door, and it warmed my heart a little when a smile lit her face at the sight of me. "Well, look at what you brought," she said, shifting her attention from me to Molly and bending down to pat the dog behind her ears. Apparently, I was chopped liver compared to a cute, furry puppy, even if said puppy was currently drooling all over my mother's shoes. I supposed I couldn't blame her; I'd fallen in love with Molly too, even though she was a handful and a half.

Besides, I was finally ghost-free, and nothing—not even the feeling of coming in second to a dog—could put a damper on my spirits, if you'll pardon the pun.

"I see she's behaving better than she was. I guess those classes I suggested are helping?" Mom said. I ignored the hint of smug in her smile.

"Is Dad home?" I asked instead, to which she nodded and motioned for me to follow her inside.

"He's in the garage," she said just as I figured it out for myself. The strains of Styx music wafted through the windows facing his workshop, and I could picture him puttering around out there. If I sneaked up on him, which was never difficult given the volume of the stereo, I might even catch him in the middle of one of his goofy dad dances. The thought brought a mischievous grin to my face, and I headed in that direction. I'd almost accomplished my mission when Molly shoved herself between me and the door and greeted Dad with a rambunctious jump that sent the paintbrush he'd been wielding skidding across the floor.

"Whoa!" Dad said, though there was more amusement than irritation in his tone. "Hello, Molly. Yes, you're a good girl, but you can't jump on people like that." He grabbed her front paws, which Molly didn't seem to appreciate, and held them there. After a minute or so, he let her go, and she kept all four feet on the floor. I tucked the technique into my mental *try it later* file, and strode across the garage to give my dad a hug.

"It's nice to see you, kiddo. I know the reason you came back to town wasn't the best, but I'm sure glad you're home. We missed you, you know." I did know, and I'd missed them as well.

Rather than get all teary-eyed, I asked my dad what he was up to and listened while he launched into an explanation. "See," he said as he led me over to his workbench, "I'm making garden fairy houses to sell on the Internet. Have you heard of Etsy? David's helping me."

I made a note to have him build one for me to give to Momma Wade. "Yeah, sure. It's all handmade stuff, and you can open your own shop and sell whatever you want, right?"

"Pretty much. Anyway, I came up with the idea because I was getting tired of my students making the same old birdhouses year after year. Industrial arts classes shouldn't be boring. I wanted to give my students more options and delve deeper into the topics of scale and design. So I came up with a simple base plan, and then tailored the embellishments to the student level. It's been such a wild success that I added a two-week module on architecture to my history classes. Not all of my history students take industrial arts classes, but those who do are getting an expanded experience."

Eager to share, he showed me the rig he'd built for creating miniature shingles and siding.

"The kids had a lot of fun with the concept, but I think I had more, so I've been building a few in my off time. David has some building experience, and when he saw what I was doing, he took an interest. Your mother told me about Etsy. I may have spent a few too many hours browsing around the site, but I decided the project might make a nice side income. I promised your mother I'd put the money towards that trip to Ireland she's been going on about for the last twenty-odd years."

My dad tends to ramble when he gets excited, and his whole face lights up. It's one of the things I love most about him.

"That's awesome, Dad," I said, examining the little houses which, I suspected, would sell like hotcakes. Each one was unique, and he'd even taken the time to craft lawn furniture out of Popsicle sticks for some of them.

I couldn't help but linger over the one with the hot pink siding, and my dad loosed another mile-wide grin. "That one's yours. For your new yard."

"It's so cute! I know exactly where I'm going to put it. Thanks, Dad." I finished admiring the fairy house just as my mother poked her head into the garage.

"I've got lunch on the table if you're hungry." She eyed Molly speculatively. "You might want to leave her in the backyard while we eat; otherwise, she's going to get fat from your father feeding her all his scraps."

I nodded my head. "Sure. I've got another hour before our class with Christine, and I'm starved."

"Perfect," she said. "I'll put a bowl of water out and make sure the gate is locked. Come on, Molly." Obediently, the dog followed her, and I suppressed an eye roll.

Over lunch, I told my parents about my new job and gave them Jacy's good news. It was nice to spend relaxed time with them for once.

This time, I came prepared for obedience class with a pocket full of treats and a *we can do this* attitude. Molly still tangled her leash around my legs, and I could hardly blame her. Now that the strings my marriage to Paul had imposed on me were ruthlessly clipped, I identified with the need to run free. Who knew there were deep, existential lessons to be learned along with the simple tenets of dog training?

"Hello everyone, I hope you're all well," Christine said at the start of the class. I'd taken a seat next to Andy and Brutus, which was probably a terrible decision since the pug and Molly couldn't seem to focus on anything else when they were near one another. Christine shot us both a glare when Brutus yipped because Molly had tangled him up in her leash.

Andy forced his dog to settle and sent half a smile in my direction, but since it lacked any real sincerity, I realized that thanks to Molly's behavior, I might have just lost the only ally I'd had.

Christine sighed but didn't comment on the disturbance, and continued explaining what the day's lesson would entail. "We've only got one class left after this, and that will be a review and assessment, so today we're going to explore the finer points of leash training. Particularly, halt and heeling with turns—that means your dog walks next to you even if you're not moving in a straight line. Then, we'll finish up with a session of red light, green light." I'd never heard that particular term, but I deduced it was something similar to a schoolyard game I used to play as a child.

"Now, our goal here is to command the dog's attention; to own his—or her—eyes and keep his gaze where *you* want it. Remember, you are the master. *You* are the alpha, and you are in charge. Naturally, your dog wants that position, and your ability to assert yourself will make all the difference." She glanced down to where Molly and Brutus were now licking each other with gusto and pursed her lips. "That might be tough for some of you, but that's why we're here. To learn how to take control so that both you and your dog are happy and in sync."

The insinuation that I was one of those people who might find cultivating obedience challenging was implied, and it irked. I set my jaw, determined to succeed today. "Come on, Molly," I murmured, "make me proud."

At Christine's instruction, we each selected a spot on the grass and walked a few yards before turning abruptly and indicating for the dog to follow. Each time Molly turned with me, I was supposed to pass her a treat, and after two perfect turns followed by two mouthfuls of beefy goodness, I thought maybe I might accomplish my goal. She really did seem to want to please. She just couldn't always remember how.

Just as I was feeling a tiny bit smug, Molly got bored with the exercise and turned back into her usual, rambunctious self. After that, every time I turned, she'd either stand still or try to move to my other side. At least I knew she was capable of following my commands; now I just had to figure out how to get her to focus.

"Everly," Christine said, interrupting my thoughts as she came toward me with that pinched look still on her face. "Why don't you let me demonstrate?" She reached for Molly's leash, which I reluctantly handed over.

"You see, it's just a matter of—whoa!" Whatever magic she'd intended on working backfired when Molly gave a fearful look and took off running, pulling Christine behind her. I choked back a laugh when her other arm pinwheeled, and she almost went, as Granny Dupree would say, ass over teakettle. With puppy energy to spare, Molly continued to zig-zag across the lawn in a desperate attempt at freedom.

"Molly," I called in a pretty close imitation of my mother. The little rascal's ears perked, and she made a mad dash back to my side, where she curled up in her favorite spot when she was feeling nervous—right behind my feet.

"Sorry about that," I said, though I didn't really mean it. To say Christine's attitude rubbed me the wrong way was the understatement of the year.

She brushed her hands off on her jeans and tossed her hair. "You certainly have your hands full with that one. It's partly breed, but mostly improper training. I'm guessing a lack of consistency on Spencer's part. I told him when he bought her that she was going to need a firm hand, and knowing how busy he was with work, I wasn't sure he could handle the responsibility. It seems I was correct."

From what I'd seen, Spencer and Molly had gotten along just fine. She and I were both simply adjusting to her new home. I kept that information to myself.

"Wait, you're the one who sold Molly to Spencer?" I asked, since it was news to me.

Christine looked at me as though I'd grown a second head. "Yes, didn't you know that? She was one of my puppies. I'm happy to take her off your hands if you don't think you're going to have the time to discipline her properly."

Maybe the idea should have appealed to me. I mean, it wasn't like I'd gone out looking for a pet; Molly had found me. But I'd already fallen in love with her, and the thought of giving her up caused a little pang in my chest. I'd only come to these classes because my mother told me I should.

"Thank you for the offer, but I don't think so," I said as politely as I could manage. "Is it true that dogs calm down once they've been neutered?."

With another purse of her lips, Christine glared at me. "That dog is an AKC registered breeder. It's unconscionable to spay her before she's fully matured. In fact, she shouldn't be spayed at all, she's meant to be bred. I realize you were not aware of Molly's value when you took her in, but you need to consider whether or not you are the right person to care for a dog of her caliber. Keep my offer in mind, Everly," she said and strode back across the lawn to finish the class.

CHAPTER 18

With Spencer gone, I could have forgotten all about him and the possibility of murder. I could have gotten on with my life. Except I'd made a promise, so I sat down and started a list of all the people I could think of who might have wanted him dead.

Since I'd barely known the man, it was a relatively short list. I put down Mrs. Lupinsky's name because she had said she wanted to kill him, and then pulled out my laptop to search for information on Cassidy Chandler because hers was the last face Spencer remembered seeing.

Even if my conscience would have let me walk away after giving him my word, Molly's presence in my house was a constant reminder. While the computer booted up, she crammed herself into the space under the desk and snuggled up with her chin resting on my foot.

"Here goes nothing." I pulled up the files I'd sent to my cloud account and did a search of all the folders in case I'd missed her name the first time. No results.

On a whim, I called Robin.

"Hey, it's Everly."

"Oh, Everly. Thank you," she said. Why was she thanking me? I had no idea, and trying to figure it out might have broken my brain. My chances of getting useful information out of her were so slim they could hide behind a needle with room to spare, but I asked anyhow.

"Um, you're welcome. I guess. Anyway, I was just checking to make sure I turned all of Spencer's files over to the correct mortgage companies, and I can't remember the phone number for one of them. I can't find it in my emails, either. You wouldn't have the number for Quantum Funding, would you?"

"Sure," she said, and then in a monotone that reminded me of Rain Man, "Quantum Funding. 343-672-56BQ17113826."

"But that's—" The call went dead. "Not even a phone number."

Not holding out any hope, I searched the cloud drive, and nearly fell out of my chair when a folder popped up in the results. Hardly breathing, I double-clicked.

When a box popped asking for a password, I felt a tingle. Finally, I was getting somewhere. Betting Spencer was a creature of habit, I typed in Molly's name, and the folder popped open to reveal five folders, and one of them had Cassidy's name on it.

Better and better.

Scanning through her files, everything looked the same to me as it had before. An application, and all the supporting documents for income. Requests and responses from various underwriters and a series of what amounted to red-stamped letters denying the loan.

By the time I had looked through all four folders, I wanted to kill Spencer myself. Or barring that, bring his ghost back so I could tell him off, then banish him all over again.

Frustrated, I stared at the screen until the words blurred, and when the headache started nagging at my temples, decided to do something proactive.

"Come on, Molly. I need to get out of here for a bit. You want to go for a walk?"

Before I had time to push back from the desk, Molly launched out of the cramped space, nearly taking my chair down on the way. It teetered on one leg just long enough to kick my heart into overdrive.

"Okay, girl. I guess that's another one of the magic words. I'll be more careful in the future." Remembering the basics from the lesson with Christine, I asked Molly to sit and waited for her to comply before I clipped on her leash.

"Christine was wrong about us, you know. We're going to make a good team once we figure each other out." I ran a hand over her sleek head and looked into those beautiful, brown eyes. "We've got this, don't we?" And then, when I opened the door, she bounded forward and dragged me down the steps. "Maybe not yet, but we're getting there."

Keeping Molly in the grassy section between the street and the sidewalk so her feet wouldn't burn on the hot pavement took plenty of patience and a lot of correction. Eventually, she caught on and settled into a pace that meant I could eat ice cream for dessert and not worry about the extra calories. An added benefit of dog ownership.

Supposedly named for the daughters of one of the first settlers in town, the four flower streets ran parallel to each other: Lilac, Primrose, Dahlia, and Tulip. We also had a set of tree streets, and another set named for types of rocks. Unimaginative, to be sure, but the town's name more than made up for the lack. I'd often wondered if the moose in question had licked the man who came up with the moniker or only the river itself.

At the end of Lilac, we went left, then left again down Primrose to begin a zig-zag pattern I planned to follow all the way to Tulip and back. Far enough, I hoped, to drain off some of Molly's excess energy. We fell into a rhythm that warmed my calf muscles and released a lovely flood of endorphins that cleared my head of all thought.

The peaceful glow lasted right up until an uneven place in the sidewalk nearly took me down. A couple of running steps and some arm-waving staved off certain disaster just as a moving van lumbered past. Another minute, and there would have been no one to witness my lack of grace.

My moment of Zen evaporated in an embarrassing cloud that lasted right up until I watched the driver try to back into the narrow driveway of the second house from the end, taking down the mailbox in the process.

Avoiding the possibility of making eye contact with anyone, I only gathered a vague impression of the place as I tried to rush past. Cute house, but small, with a porch spanning the narrow front, and trim the same sunny yellow color I'd wanted to paint my kitchen.

Molly, however, decided the bashed in mailbox now lying near the sidewalk constituted some sort of threat. Fur standing up in a ridge along her spine, she growled menacingly, and I had to drag her away, but not before I noted the number on the side.

Someone was either moving into or out of 116 Tulip Street.

With Molly still keyed up from her encounter with the invisible mailbox demon, I abandoned my plan to weave back through the streets the way I had come, and instead, followed Pleasant Street all the way back to where my house sat on the corner of Lilac. Molly had calmed after a few minutes, but I couldn't stop wondering why that address seemed so familiar.

Then it hit me. Leo and his porch railing.

Then it hit me even harder. 116 Tulip Street was the current address in one of the folders I'd been scanning right before I went for a walk. Cassidy Chandler's to be exact.

Cassidy was Leo's tenant. Or she had been until Spencer got her into a mortgage, anyway.

The timing was right since the papers had been signed mere hours before Spencer was killed. There had to be a connection, but no matter how I reasoned it out, I couldn't see a solid motive for Cass to commit murder.

If Spencer had died before closing on her house, that would be a different story, but why would she kill him after he'd made her dream of homeownership a reality? The only person who wouldn't benefit from the deal was Leo Hanson, who was about to lose a tenant. One who was moving, most likely, without giving her landlord the required thirty day's notice.

Could mild-mannered Leo be a killer?

Anyone could kill given the right provocation. But was the loss of a single tenant enough to tip a man over the edge?

Not Leo. Not the man who pined after a woman for years because he couldn't get up the gumption to ask her out. I just couldn't see him mustering up the passion for committing murder.

Still, Leo couldn't be the only person who owned rental property in town. Maybe Spencer had poached one too many tenants. Or he had more than one enemy among those who got turned down. Desperate people do horrible things. Ray Watson proved that when he killed Hudson Montayne for not letting his son play baseball on a particular day. Even Brian Dean had been driven to the edge of his tether by the financial and mental stress of not getting a mortgage.

Following that train of thought, I hurried Molly along. As soon as I got home, I scanned through the folders for the most recent rejections. Only one name popped besides Jacy and Brian in the past six months. Milo Lynch worked at Cappy's Tavern. His name went on the list.

Logically, if I were going to look at landlords, I would find my suspect among the most recent transactions, and I would be looking for someone who had lost multiple tenants. Spencer worked with mortgage applicants from the five smaller towns in the area, and occasionally some from farther out.

But, I figured I could rule out anyone not from Mooselick River because the killer had known enough about the recycling center to lure Spencer in there at just the right time.

Huffing out a breath, I calculated the odds anyone could have known the exact minute the chute would open at somewhere around nine hundred and eleventy million to one. It had to be an accident.

It couldn't be an accident, or Spencer wouldn't have haunted me.

Unless … maybe he'd been knocked out or drugged and dragged into the recycling center. If so, I'd still be looking at someone who knew he'd be buried under a mountain of paper, but the timing wouldn't have to be so precise. Someone from town, though. Definitely someone who knew how the system worked.

There was no way to know who might or might not have that kind of information at the ready, so I'd need to concentrate on motive first, then see about means and opportunity. And since Spencer hadn't had much going for him in the personal-relationships department, and I didn't think Robin was smart enough to contemplate murder, that put me right back to looking through the files, but at least I had a clearer head about why and what to look for: disgruntled landlords.

To that end, I printed out a list of closings for the past six months and began to cross off possibilities, starting with those that weren't local. The resulting list was pretty short, and it included three of the homes financed by Quantum Funding. It gave me enough of a tingle that I added the other two.

I caught Mrs. Tipton in the act of locking up the town office ten minutes ahead of closing. "I'm sorry, Martha, but I'd like to look at the property tax evaluations for last year. They're a matter of public record, aren't they?"

She heaved a sigh. "They are, yes, but I'm closing up early today. Come back tomorrow, please."

"It's important. I wouldn't bother you otherwise." I waved my list in her face. "What can you tell me about the previous owners of these seven homes?"

Faster than I'd have given her credit for being able to move, Martha snatched the list out of my hand and picked up a pen. "This one was an outta-stater. Bought the place with the idea of moving here when he retired. Looks like he changed his mind. This one, well, that's a story. Billy Thomas thought he was going to make himself a fortune flipping houses. Bought this one for forty thousand, put another twenty grand into it, and sold it for seventy-five. By the time he paid the real estate fees, he came out of the deal with less than a thousand dollars, and that was the end if his flipping career."

Cross those two off the list. "And the others?"

"That's easy. Leo Hanson owned the lot of them. Now, if you don't mind, I'd like to get to my hair appointment ahead of that Bess Tate. She takes the good chair if she gets there first, and I don't want to be stuck with the lumpy one."

Dumbstruck, I stepped back and let her close the door.

Leo Hanson had just jumped to the top of my list of suspects. All two of them.

CHAPTER 19

A gentle breeze fluttered the sheer curtains but failed to cool the upstairs corner bedroom. Inspired by Neena's declaration that she was going to live her life come what may, I had decided to take control of the main part of the house by clearing out the rest of Catherine's things.

Besides, I needed something to take my mind off of murder for a day.

Choosing the smallest bedroom to start my cleaning and clearing project seemed like a good idea at the time. Even shoved against the wall, the double bed took up most of the space, leaving only a narrow walkway between it and the three dressers lining the opposite wall.

Three dressers and one of them was small. How bad could it be?

I'd forgotten to factor in Catherine's talent for making use of every molecule of space.

The top drawer of the oak dresser was like a history lesson on nylons starting with seven unopened packages of silk stockings—the kind that whispered between the fingers and required garters. Very sexy, and not at all the right type of thing to put on the charity table at the yard sale.

I set them aside and reached back in for the next evolution in hosiery—the kind that came in a plastic egg. Several of those were still sealed in the original packaging, and they joined the silk ones in the decide-later pile. But the two that had been opened felt heavier than the rest. Curious, I decided to look inside.

First, let me say, I will never understand the thought process behind that particular brand of packaging. Were they trying to say the pantyhose were hatched by some weird, nylon chicken? Or was it supposed to make adult women think they were getting a prize from one of those plug-in-a-quarter candy machines?

Either way, the egg was too big to grip comfortably, and slippery besides. Somewhere between the stages of finding the debacle amusing and being tempted to wing the stupid thing against the wall, I got the bright idea to try and crack it like an actual egg. Didn't work. But setting it on a flat surface and pushing down on it did. The two halves squashed and fell open to reveal a wad of cash, rolled up and held with a dried-up rubber band that fell to pieces in my hand.

Oh, Catherine.

It was one thing to get the house so cheaply, and I understood the number of reasons the town had let it go for next to nothing. It was quite another to end up with a car and find out most of the furniture in the place carried a decent value, but finding actual money threw me. I knew I should be grateful and thank my lucky stars that Catherine had had no heirs. After reading part of one of her diaries, it only made me sad.

What would make her stash away money this way? She had to have had plenty, or she could never have collected so many things. The roll of ones and fives equaled out to a little over a hundred dollars.

Just as I pressed my hand down on the second egg, my phone rang.

"I have news." Patrea didn't bother with hello. "And speaking of, why did I see your face in the paper? Didn't I tell you not to talk to reporters?"

"I didn't."

She harrumphed.

"I really didn't. Okay, I was there at the time, and I did say some things, and he did take our picture. But I never said a word about Paul or his family. Just about the town yard sale. We're trying to create some buzz around the event and divert some of the tourist traffic that normally takes the bypass."

Patrea didn't sound as if she cared. "Don't do it again. Now, for my news, and you're not going to like it because I sent copies of some pages of your prenuptial agreement to my handwriting guy."

Now it was my turn to harrumph.

127

"You're a good one to lecture me about a little article in the local paper when you're going behind my back after I told you I didn't want to pursue anything to do with that agreement."

"Okay, fine. If you don't want to hear the results—"

Did I? After a second to think about it, I decided I did.

"You wouldn't be calling me unless there was a reason, and you already said it was bad news, so you might as well get it over with."

"The results aren't one hundred percent since I only gave him copies to work from, but he said it was clear Paul forged your signature on at least two pages of the prenup. If you let me have the originals, I can prove to the court that he cheated you out of a portion of the marital assets. Now, will you let me go after your ex? What he's done isn't just reprehensible on a personal level, it's a misdemeanor."

The mental image of Paul behind bars wasn't wholly unsatisfying. I had, after all, caught him in bed with my former best friend, so picturing him in prison-orange brought a little surge of triumph.

And yet, I sighed. "We both know his family will find a way to get him off the hook, and I'll come off looking like some blood-sucking leech." Patrea started to speak, but I talked over her. "Which wouldn't bother me in the least as far as that goes. I'm not worried about my reputation."

"Then let me pursue this."

"I wasn't finished. Whether or not there's any truth to the rumors about the Hasting's charitable contributions, I helped raise a lot of money for good causes, and people in need benefited from the work. Maybe not as much as they should have, but when the alternative is nothing, no amount is too little. If I go after Paul, I might as well put a target on my own back, and since my only monetary connection to the family had to do with the foundation, the best way to retaliate is through the charity work I've done for them. So, as much as I'd like to see Paul get what he has coming, I'd rather not jeopardize any of the programs the family is regularly funding just because my ego took a hit."

Now Patrea sighed. "You're right. I know you are. But you have to promise me that if we find that they really were cheating the charities out of money, you'll let me take them down before they drag your name through the mud."

"You have my word. Now, on a different topic, you read about the town-wide yard sale. You should come. You never know, I might be willing to part with that occasional table you wanted."

"I'll think about it." She disconnected without saying goodbye.

Before I put the phone down, I tagged Jacy.

"You're off tomorrow, right?" Wednesday was her typical day off. "What are you doing later?"

"Sitting on the couch, binging Netflix while Brian swears he's awake between snores. Typical Tuesday."

"You up for a girl's night out at Cappy's? I'll see if Neena wants to come. You can be the designated driver, and I'll buy you all the virgin daiquiris you can drink." As long as they were served by Milo Lynch so I could ask him a few questions.

CHAPTER 20

Milo Lynch hadn't killed Spencer. I figured that out within fifteen minutes at Cappy's Tavern.

Decked out to resemble an old-time saloon, the decor relied heavily on scarred but polished wood, bat-wing doors, and dim lighting furnished by flicker bulbs strung through old wagon wheels.

Jacy picked a booth with a view of the dance floor, but far enough back to be shielded from some of the noise.

Neena slid in first. "You're sure it doesn't look like I'm on the prowl?"

Wearing a shapeless tee at least two sizes too big, a pair of ratty jeans, a messy bun, and not a stitch of makeup, Neena couldn't have looked less open for business.

Then again, who was I to talk? I hadn't paid much more attention to my attire than Neena. My jeans weren't ripped, and my tee fit better, but I wasn't wearing makeup, and my hair was a disaster from the humidity. Plus, I wasn't Jacy, who could wear the bag her clothes came in and still manage to look stylish.

"No, I think you're fine." Given the size of the Tuesday night crowd, she could have shown up in her nightgown and slippers and not created a stir.

"Hey, Milo." Jacy greeted the very man I'd come to see. "How's married life treating you?"

Round face splitting in a grin, he said, "Happy wife, happy life. We went to Niagara Falls for the honeymoon. That's where my parents went, so we followed tradition. Spent a week there, and took in a show at the casino. Then we drove down to the Poconos and spent a week in the same hotel Jayme's parents stayed in on their honeymoon. We just got back on Friday."

By my calculations, Milo had been out of town on the day of Spencer's death. Now, I was down to Mrs. Lupinsky, whom I'd never considered as a serious contender, and Leo Hanson.

"Congratulations!" I said.

"Thanks! What can I getcha?"

"Wings sampler—double sized—and one of everything off the appetizer menu," Jacy ordered for the table before Neena or I had a chance to look at a menu. "What?" she said when she saw our faces. "It's a bar. You come to a bar, you eat bar food. You weren't planning to order salads, were you? Besides, you'll get celery with the wings if you absolutely have to have rabbit food."

"Not all of us are eatin' for two." Neena softened the comment with a smile. "But they do have good wings here, so I'm not complainin'." She poured beer from a pitcher of draft into the frosted glass Milo had set in front of her and took a healthy sip. "Not bad for off the tap."

We talked about everything and nothing until Milo brought out enough food to feed an army. "Jeez, Jace. Are you sure you're not eating for six?"

"I hope not, but my aunt had twins, so you never know. I could be eating for three. It's too early to tell, but wouldn't that be something?"

Since Jacy grinned, Neena raised her beer mug. "A toast to the possibility."

It was the first of too many toasts that evening.

Halfway through my second drink, I recognized the couple in the booth across the way, and my mouth fell open. "You've got to be kidding me."

"What?" Jacy swiveled to look in the direction I was looking. "What? I don't see anything."

"That's Robin, and she's draped over Ernie Polk tighter than plastic wrap on a sandwich. Isn't he married?"

Jacy looked at me funny. "I forgot you've been gone a while. He was, but his wife left him two, maybe three years back. Rumors flew, but I never heard exactly why. Maybe he had a thing for little girls. Robin's young enough to be his daughter."

Neena leaned to look past Jacy. "Well, she's not acting like a daughter now."

131

"No, she is not. Ernie didn't waste much time moving in on her, now did he?" Maybe he was the one who killed Spencer. Despite the alcohol fogging my brain, I remembered him telling me all about how the paper shredder worked, so he had the means. Wanting Robin for himself spoke to motive, and he most likely had the opportunity. Had the whole murder trifecta been staring me in the face this whole time? "Do you think he had the hots for her while she was still burning up the sheets with Spencer?"

Jacy snorted some virgin daiquiri up her nose and went into a coughing fit over that one.

"Ernie moving in on Robin. Are you kidding me with that?" she said when she got herself under control. "The only man slower than Ernie to declare his intentions in this town is Leo Hanson. If you put the pair of them in a race with a glacier, the glacier would win. Hands down. Trust me. She made the first move. She probably made all the moves."

The second margarita had greased my tongue more than expected. "Pfft. Men are pigs. She might have made the moves, but the minute she let him know she was interested his brain shut off and hormones took over."

It wasn't the words, but the venom in my tone that made Jacy look at me with sympathy, and I got annoyed.

"Oh, I know Brian's not a pig, and Hudson had his faults, but he was a good man," I said, waving them off. "Just don't go thinking they're all like that. There's plenty of scumbags out there. Even the ones who are all polished up and slick looking on the surface."

I don't drink a lot, and for good reason. I'm a lightweight.

Tequila loosened the reins on my temper, and it was big enough that I let slip that Patrea was fairly certain Paul had forged some parts of the prenuptial agreement.

"That lying, cheating, lowlife, no good, piece of crap on a cracker," Jacy growled. "I never could stand the man. You're going to go after him, aren't you?"

"You should." Neena shredded a wing viciously. "Take him apart. He's earned it."

"Patrea wants to yank his danglers up over his head, and I'm more inclined by the day to tell her to go ahead and do it, but I'm not sure if I want to take it that far."

"Don't tell me you're still in love with him."

Taking a moment to think about my answer, I dipped a fried mushroom in marinara sauce, bit it in half, and chewed slowly.

"I've thought a lot about my feelings for Paul, and to be perfectly honest, I don't think I was ever that much in love with him. At first, it was exciting. Here was this man who was used to getting what he wanted, and what he said he wanted was me. It made me feel special and cherished."

Jacy pointed at me with a mozzarella stick. "That's how he hooked you, but for him, it was all about the thrill of the chase."

"I suppose so, but once he caught me, he decided he owned me, and everything changed. He turned into someone else, and to be honest, I'm not all that sorry it's over. He wasn't the love of my life, and I like the life I'm building here. It feels pretty good to be alone right now."

"Well, I hate it," Neena said. "I'm happy you're doing well alone, but I hate every little minute of it."

Jacy reached over to pat her hand.

Neena looked down into her beer glass like it had the answers to the universe. "Hudson had his faults, but he was a good husband most of the time, and I can't help wondering if he'd still be alive if I hadn't sent him away over something so stupid."

"Or you'd both be dead. Don't forget, Ray came after me, and that time, it was premeditated."

"Maybe so. But I can tell you this, I don't like being alone, but I'll never find another man like my Hudson." A tear slid down Neena's cheek, thereby cementing our drinking roles. She was the one who would get sloppy and cry, and I was the one with the temper.

"I'll tell you what. We can be old maids together. We'll be the old aunties for those six kids Jacy's carrying."

"Come on. Don't jinx me like that. Besides, I'm going to make a prediction." Jacy's voice went all solemn. "Five years from tonight, we will come back here and have a drink, and I predict that both of you will have found love."

"Calling BS on that," Neena said and rolled her eyes. "I'm off the market. Off. The. Market."

"Naw." I pointed a thumb at Jacy. "She rarely makes predictions, but they always come true."

"They do not." Jacy balled up a napkin and threw it at me, but without any heat behind it. "You take that back. My mother's the one with the woo woo tendencies."

"They do, too. Did you or did you not predict I'd throw up on my shoes when we stole that bottle of wine from under your mother's sink?"

"Oh, like that wasn't an easy one to see coming."

"And didn't you predict you were going to marry Brian in sixth grade when he put gum in your hair?"

"Okay, maybe I did do that." Jacy caved. "Fine then, that just means I'm right, and you'll both have happy relationships in your future."

The lights were dim, but still bright enough to see the expression on Neena's face, and I had to look away or give in to the urge to snort.

After one more round, Jacy declared she'd had enough, and dragged us out of there.

134

CHAPTER 21

At somewhere around a quarter to nine the next morning, according to a slit-eyed glance at my bedside clock, Armageddon occurred.

Okay, that's an exaggeration. Armageddon didn't actually occur, it just felt like it did when Molly licked my bare foot and I jumped. The motion set off thunder in my head, and lightning in my belly.

Who had been mixing the drinks the night before? Satan?

When she whined, my head threatened to split right in two.

"I'm up. I'm up." Almost true. I'd managed to rise to a sitting position without actually dying. "Next chance I get, I'm installing a pet door."

The trip to let her out didn't kill me, even if I wished it would, and neither did the one to the bathroom where the life-giving painkillers lived.

"I am never drinking with Neena again," I said to no one, then groaned when my text alert went off at roughly the same volume as a bomb blast.

Come to the diner. I have the cure for what ails you, Jacy had written.

I doubted that, but managed to get Molly fed, throw on some clothes, and was just walking out my front door when I saw Neena step out hers.

What does it say about me that I was glad to see her looking nearly as bad as I felt?

"You going to the diner?"

"Jacy. Text. Hangover cure. Must have. Might die." Neena tried to put words together.

We stood there like a pair of zombies, debating if either one of us was fit to drive when I saw a flash of pink, and then Jacy's smiling face beamed out at me from behind the wheel of her Jeep.

"Get in. I'm on break, and I only have ten minutes."

I did, but only because my brain hadn't yet engaged enough to remember that Jacy drove like a maniac. Neena settled in the back, no easy feat even with the top off, and huddled there staring at the go cup Jacy had handed her.

"Drink up. You'll feel better."

Unless the contents of that cup were made from magic, I doubted her word, but since I couldn't think of a good reason not to, I took a pull on the straw. And then I lost the will to speak.

Neena, however, did not. "What the world is in this?"

"At home, I'd use a sports drink, but I was at work, so I had to go with the next best thing. It's pickle juice, a little hair of the dog, and tummy tablets, you know, the fizzy kind. Full of electrolytes and stuff. Fix you right up."

"Hair of the dog?" I asked, trying not to gag.

"Mabel keeps a jar of moonshine in her desk. I threw in a little slug."

"Oh, I thought it was paint thinner."

"I'm going to die. I'm going to throw up, and then I'm going to die." Neena did not die, and neither did I. Cautiously, I took another sip, and then a third.

"It's disgusting, but I think I feel a little better." Probably the painkillers kicking in and not the pickle juice cocktail.

When I looked up, we'd pulled in behind the diner.

"A few more sips of the cure and something to eat, and you'll be right as rain. I promise."

We followed her through the back door, and by the time we settled into a corner booth, my stomach had settled, and my head only throbbed when Jacy swung by wearing a perky smile or chirped a greeting to a new customer.

"You hate her a little, too?" Neena picked up a triangle slice of toast and bit off a corner. When it didn't appear to insult her alcohol-ravaged stomach, she doused her eggs with ketchup and tucked in.

"She's my best friend in the world, but right now ... maybe a little."

Leo Hanson walked through the door as I used my fork to scoop the last of my eggs onto a bit of toast. "There's Leo, I think he might have—" I caught myself just in time to change the end of that sentence. "—a thing for Mabel. Keep an eye on him, you'll see." Mostly I wanted an excuse to watch him without it looking weird to Neena. He hadn't seen us, I didn't think.

What I expected him to do, I'm not sure. He wasn't likely to jump up and try to kill someone right there in the diner. I blamed the hint of moonshine in Jacy's hangover cure for the flight of fancy. But the man looked harmless to me; like a human bunny or something.

"You're right. Look how he watches her, but not in a creepy, stalkerish way." Neena dabbed a bit of ketchup off her lip. "She knows it, too."

"Really? How can you tell?" As far as I could see, Mabel treated Leo with the same detachment that kept most people at bay. When she set a finished order in the window, her eyes passed over him without lingering. "I don't see it. She's hardly glanced at him once this whole time. She never pays attention to him."

"Don't look at the face, look at the body language. As soon as he walked in, her center of gravity lowered. She's looser in the hips, and she's arching her back, so it perks her boobs up."

I almost snorted my coffee, but then I looked. "You're right. It's subtle, but her posture's different." Now that she pointed it out, the signs were obvious.

The dance was delicate, barely a flutter, and could end abruptly should either party get tired of the turtle-paced speed at which it progressed. Mabel and Leo were inching their way toward something, though. A man with the patience for plodding along with the love of his life wasn't likely to kill over the need to find a new tenant. Unless he was, and my sense of him was way off.

I had to know, so I excused myself to Neena and made my way to his table.

"Hey, Leo." He was, after all, my new employer, and hadn't bothered to provide me with a whole lot of the information I felt necessary to do the job. What better time than right now to clear up a few questions? "You mind if I join you for a minute? We can talk about my new duties as your property manager."

With difficulty, he tore his eyes away from Mabel. "What do you need to know?"

"For starters, I'll need a list of tenants and addresses. Spencer didn't keep that information on the office computer system. Don't you think that's odd?"

Leo shrugged. "He got the job done."

"It looks like Spencer helped Cassidy Chandler get a mortgage, so she's moving out of the unit on Tulip Street. You must be annoyed because she didn't give you enough notice to find a new tenant. Do want me to take out an ad or did you have someone else lined up already?" I leaned in and watched his reaction closely. He took his time answering, and I wondered if asking had put a target on my back.

"I guess if you're going to work for me, there are some things you need to know. We'll talk, but not here. Too many prying ears in this place. I like to keep my business to myself. Why don't we take a walk?"

"Okay. Just let me tell my friends I'm leaving." *In case you are a dirty killer, and you get any ideas about taking me out.*

Now I faced a dilemma. I hadn't told anyone my suspicions for a couple of reasons. I was the only one who knew Spencer's death wasn't an accident, and I didn't want to reveal how I knew it wasn't. Jacy might believe the ghost story. She'd never look at me the same way again, but she might believe me. She would not, I didn't think, buy Leo as a killer. Besides, she was busy with a table of tourists.

"I'm going to be doing some work for Mr. Hanson," I said to Neena. "He's asked me to have a word with him in private. Can you keep an eye out for us, and if I'm not back in a few minutes, come rescue me? He can be a bit of a talker once you get him going."

"Okay, but I'm taking your coffee refill."

Leo paid his tab, and I breathed a sigh of relief when he circled the diner and headed for the picnic table where Mabel and the rest of the staff took their breaks.

"How much do you know about Quantum Funding?" Leo looked at me intently.

The true answer was both more and less than he thought, but I played off the question. "Only that when Cassidy and four other of your tenants were turned down for conventional options, Spencer

138

went to a private lender. I don't know if that lender is on the up and up, and I also know there's no way Cassidy gave thirty days notice."

Then I had a derp moment. "But Spencer knew, and since he's managing the property, he probably already had a tenant lined up. And he did the same for the other tenants as well." Leo's motive just went poof, and I felt like an idiot for cooking up something so flimsy, to begin with.

He pushed his glasses up and looked at me for a moment then nodded to himself. "If you're going to work for me, you might as well know all the facts. But first, give me your word that what I'm about to tell you stays between us. If this gets out, I'll be hounded all over town."

"I promise that whatever you tell me goes into the vault."

"Quantum Funding is perfectly legitimate. I know, because I *am* Quantum Funding."

A butterfly flapping its wings could have blown me off the bench.

"You're Quantum Funding." I did some quick mental math. "You put up financing for five homes? Even with down payments, and house prices being low in the area, you had to be looking at over three-quarters of a million dollars." That was a chunk of money to have available.

"A penny saved is a penny earned, but a penny properly invested is a penny earning dividends. I've always had a knack for turning pennies into dollars."

"And Spencer talked you into investing in more real estate."

Leo's fist hit the table, and I jumped half out of my skin. He pointed his finger at me. "No. That's where you're wrong. I invested in people. Good people who had made some financial mistakes in the past, but were turning it all around. Just not fast enough to suit the bank. I invested in tenants who had never missed a rent check, and who were diligent in caring for my property."

I'd never seen Leo this animated. This was a Leo I could get on board with. One who might actually have a shot at talking Mabel into a date.

"I invested in people who needed me. I'll make a decent return on the money, but more, I'll know I made a difference in their lives because I believed in them." Who knew the man had that much passion simmering under the surface?

"Everyone needs someone to take a chance on them at least once in their lives."

Tears burned, and I laid a hand on the fist that still rested on the table. "You're one hell of a man, Leo. I'm proud to know you. Is Mabel aware of your altruistic streak?"

Face burning, Leo cleared his throat. "Wouldn't be true altruism if I ran around bragging on myself, now would it? You come back tomorrow and I'll have some paperwork for you to sign. You can pick up your first paycheck on Friday."

I couldn't help myself—I went around the table and kissed him on the cheek. "Mabel's an idiot if she doesn't snap you up, you know."

CHAPTER 22

Even the air in town felt festive when the day of the big yard sale dawned with blue skies and scorching sun despite the weather forecaster predicting early morning rain. Word had spread among the network of food truck owners, and if one more showed up, I wasn't sure where we would put them.

I'd been up since six to help with the final preparations, which included getting Dani and her ponies settled into the parking lot near Mabel's diner while Martha, Bess, and Patricia handled the petting zoo.

The signs were up, the items priced, and the Presbyterians and Methodists had both come out in force, their charity tables facing off across the street from each other.

"I can't thank you enough for all you've done, Everly," Martha practically gushed. "Mooselick River thanks you."

"You're welcome. Now that you ladies have everything under control, I'll see you later." I had my own yard sale items to finish setting up. Except when I stepped up onto the front porch, the thought of making a little extra money went right out of my head.

My front door hung slightly ajar, and for the life of me, I couldn't remember if I'd locked it before I left.

"Molly!" I called, but she didn't come running like she normally did. "Where are you, you silly dog? Are you hiding under the bed again?" Not a peep out of her.

She wasn't in the bedroom or in any of the open upstairs rooms. Frantic, I made a second round of all the rooms, including checking under the beds. There was no sign of her.

I must have left the door unlocked, and now Molly was gone.

Feeling like there was a twenty-pound weight in the pit of my stomach, I traced the path we always took on our walks, calling to her the whole way, listening for her happy bark.

Precious minutes slid past before I headed home and got in my car to widen the search.

By now, all my hard PR work and the signs along the highway had begun to do their job. Mooselick River was filling up with bargain hunters. Traffic inched down the streets, but I managed to veer around most of it and head out toward where Spencer had lived—watching along the side of the road in case the worst had happened.

It occurred to me that Momma Wade relieving me of Spencer's presence didn't mean he'd actually left the area. Molly might still see him if he was hanging around. It would be just like him to lure her away in an attempt to get me to do his bidding now that he couldn't harass me anymore.

The only thing moving near his old place was the for sale sign swinging on the breeze. I tried the recycling center next, and after calling for Molly in vain, I sat in my car and cried.

Traffic on the way back was worse than when I'd left town. At any other time, I'd have felt pretty good about myself for generating so much publicity for the yard sale. But not when I needed to find my dog. Moving at a snail's pace, it took forever to get back as far as the grocery store.

After a minute of not moving close enough to pull into the parking lot, I took drastic measures. Something on Sally's undercarriage dragged bottom when her wheels jumped the curb, then I zipped down behind the loading docks.

At the end of the lot, I whispered my apologies to the owner of the house next door and drove over their lawn. I made it almost all the way to Jacy's house before the traffic forced me to pull over and abandon my car.

"Jace!" I yelled and interrupted her in the middle of a yard sale transaction. She couldn't have looked more surprised to see me running down the sidewalk.

"What's wrong? You look just awful."

"I feel just awful. Molly's gone. I got home from the set-up meeting this morning, and the door was open. She's nowhere in the house."

I expected some sympathy, an offer of help, and maybe a hug from Jacy. Instead, she jumped to her feet and shook me so hard, my teeth rattled together.

"What were you thinking?" she demanded. "You come home and see the front door open, you assume you've had a break-in, and you don't go in the house. This is not rocket science, Ev. It's just common sense."

"Okay, I deserved that. But Molly's gone, and I have to find her."

Not missing a beat, Jacy called to Brian. "I gotta go. Take over for me." Anyone else might have suggested Molly would return on her own, but Jacy could see I needed to search.

"She could be anywhere."

Except she wasn't. My feet ached, and my throat was sore from calling her by the time we gave up and went back to my place in case she'd wandered back there while we were looking. I went into the bathroom and resorted to the one source I had that might be able to help.

"Spencer, if you can hear me, I need your help. Come back. I want you to haunt me. Please. Just help me find Molly."

Utter silence met my plea. Momma Wade had well and truly banished Spencer from my life. Just when I needed him most, and it was all my fault.

I knew what I needed to do.

Jacy sat at the kitchen table with a glass of ice water dripping a pool of condensation in front of her when I took the opposite chair.

"I have to tell you something, and it's going to sound crazy."

"You do remember who my mother is, don't you?" She didn't grin because the situation was dire, but her eyes sparkled.

"Funny you should mention your mom."

I launched into the story of what had happened after the day at the lake.

"You've been haunted twice now, and you didn't tell me?" Her annoyed look made me squirm in my chair.

"I was hoping you wouldn't pick up on that particular part of the story."

"Well, I did. Why didn't you say anything?" she said. "Did you think I wouldn't believe you? Or that I'd think any less of you because something weird happened?"

"Maybe. A little. Can you blame me? It sounds pretty out there."

I watched her face as she sorted through the details of my story, and then her lips quirked into a smile. "Hudson nailed Ray Watson with a mannequin head. How could I not believe you? No one in their right mind would make up something like that."

"No, I suppose not, and I appreciate you thinking I'm in my right mind. I guess we need to call your mom and see if she can help."

Jacy made the call and put her mom on speaker, but Leandra could only repeat what she'd told me when I came to her. What she'd done to me had been an accident, but the reversal hadn't been, and she'd warned me it would be final before we started. There was nothing she could to for me now.

"You'd need to contact him through other sources. A medium, or—"

"—or an Ouija board. Would that work?" Jacy was thinking clearer than I was.

"It should if he's still in the area, but there might be repercussions for you, Everly. I can't say for sure what would happen if you open that door." Jacy left the table.

"It's a chance I'll take. Molly's missing, and I can't say why, but I'm positive Spencer is the only one who can find her." Every cell in my body insisted Molly needed finding and soon. "Thanks for the advice, Momma Wade. We'll let you know if it pans out." I punched the button to end the call and heard a muted thump coming from the living room, followed by a few choice words.

Ouija board in hand, Jacy met me halfway to the living room. "Don't look. I had a mishap with the board game filing system. We'll clean it up later; let's just get this done."

Because it seemed the right thing to do, we settled cross-legged on the carpet.

"I feel like I'm fourteen at a sleepover. Are you sure this is going to work?"

Jacy gave me a level look. "Until today, I didn't believe my mother talked to actual spirit guides or that ghosts were real. I'm starting to rethink my stance on the Easter bunny, so if you're looking for a rational answer to that question, you might be doomed to disappointment."

"Fair enough." I put my fingertips on the planchette then pulled them back. "Should we light candles or something?"

144

"It's broad daylight. What would be the point?"

"Okay. Just let me settle my mind a bit." I breathed in and out a few times until I felt calmer and reached out again. "Spencer Charles, if you can hear me, can you just, you know, make this thing move or something."

"Real spooky, Ev."

"What? It's not like I'm an expert on Ouija etiquette or attracting ghosts."

The planchette moved. I yanked my fingers back, and so did Jacy. Some ghost hunters we'd make.

"Put your fingers back on there," Jacy said.

"Why, it's moving by itself."

"What's it saying?"

I leaned forward for a closer look just as the planchette flew off the board. It slammed me right in the forehead. Not hard enough to knock me out, but still, that was the last thing I remembered until I woke up with Jacy's face so close it looked like a blur.

"What are you doing?"

"Shut up. I was checking to see if you were breathing." She leaned back a little, and her eyes came into focus. Relief spread over her pale face.

"Oh, I thought you were trying to wake me up with a kiss or something."

"You know I love you, but only as a friend."

I sat up. "What happened?"

Spencer, fully visible now, answered. "You passed out. Can we get on with things already? I know where Molly is."

"Where is she? Is she okay?" Feeling only slightly woozy, I scrambled up from the floor.

Even though I'd told her the whole story, I don't think Jacy believed it until I started talking to thin air.

She was looking around, trying to find the source of the other side of my conversation. "Um, is he here?"

"You can't see him?"

"No, she can't," Spencer snapped. "Why are you wasting time? We need to get out to Christine Murray's place and rescue Molly."

"She's at Christine's? How did she get there? At least she's safe."

Jacy started to say something, but I held up a hand for her to stop when Spencer's face turned thunderous.

"When someone steals your dog and locks her up in a cage out behind the barn, what makes you assume the dog is safe?"

Translating from ghost to actual vocals, I said, "He says Christine Murray stole Molly, and that we need to go rescue her."

"Does he realize traffic is backed up for miles?"

Spencer huffed. "She doesn't have to act like I'm not here."

"To her, you're not." I felt like a ping pong ball. "He wants you to talk to him."

Jacy turned to an empty spot nowhere near where Spencer hovered. "Sorry, this is my first time being around the um—" she turned to me, "what do I call him? He's not undead ... fleshly challenged."

"Can we forget about semantics?" Spencer's temper heated up enough to cool the room. "And get moving?"

"I'd say chill out, but that's an oxymoron with you."

Goosebumps pebbled Jacy's arms. "Is he doing that? I'm officially creeped out. Should we call Ernie and report Christine?"

I thought about it for a few seconds, then shook my head. "I can't exactly tell him how I know what happened. We'll just go talk to her and make sure Molly's there first. I wouldn't want to get her into trouble based on a misunderstanding."

Between having to dodge slow-moving vehicles and foot traffic, the ten-minute walk back to Jacy's house took twenty. I considered an attempt at annoying Spencer just to get a break from the heat and humidity.

"This is nuts," I said when we got to my car, and it was still blocked in. According to Spencer, Christine lived just a couple of miles from his place, but that meant we'd have to drive right through the worst of the traffic. "We'd get there faster walking."

"No, we won't. Come on." Jacy dragged me toward her place. "I have a better idea."

"Another cross-country shortcut in the Jeep?" Situated where it was, Jacy's place bordered an embankment that dropped down to the railroad tracks.

146

"Can't. I sold it last night. This is just as good, though. Wait here." She practically danced her way up the driveway, and plopped a kiss on her husband's cheek, then said something to him in too low a voice for me to hear. Brian's gaze flicked toward me, then back to her, and I could see the moment he decided to go along with whatever she was asking.

Jacy clapped her hands, and Brian pulled something out of his pocket, and reluctantly passed it to her.

"Come on." She turned and motioned for me to follow her as she disappeared around the corner of the one-up, one-down apartment building. She was just settling into the seat of a six-wheel, side-by-side deathtrap of an ATV. "Get in. It belongs to Brian's dad, but he won't mind if we use it."

Reluctantly, I did as she said. "You know how to drive this thing, right?"

"Sure. It's easy."

With that, she gunned the engine and sent a shower of gravel spurting out behind us. I grabbed onto the roll bar and said a hasty prayer when she directed the machine across the back lawn, then ripped left to follow a trail along the edge of the drop-off.

I glanced right only once, then focused my attention on Jacy. She grinned as she drove.

"I've seen that look on your face before, you know," I said then wished I hadn't when she took her eyes off the trail to look at me. "It's the same one you used to get on the bumper cars at the fair."

She shot me a sideways grin. "Hang on."

The next thing I knew, we were headed down the side of the embankment. I didn't have time to work up a proper panic before we leveled out again.

"This trail runs right out to the lake, but there's a turn-off not too far ahead that comes out behind the recycling center. Track's rough but passable."

Some of Spencer's urgency had finally translated to me. "How long will it take to get there?"

"Not long now. There's the sign."

Barely slowing, we turned left again.

"Uh, Jace. That sign was for snowmobiles, not ATVs."

147

"You want to get there or not? Relax and enjoy the ride. I know what I'm doing."

As much as I could, I took her advice. The canopy of trees dripped sun dapples among the shady spots, and the air smelled richly of moss and moist soil. The serenity lulled me as we bumped over the rough terrain.

"You know, this is actually fun. I might want to get one of these eventually."

I kept that thought right up until we rocketed across a bridge barely wider than the span of the wheels and all the blood in my body headed for my feet.

Up another hill, the ground leveled out, and when we broke through the tree line, the roof of the recycling shed popped into view not too far away. We got close enough to see a bustle of activity, and I made out Ron Murray's figure in the distance before Jacy veered right and brought us out on a track running alongside the road.

"This trail runs out past Barrow quarry, which is right across the road from the Murray farm. How do you want to play this? Walk right up to the front door and demand she give you your dog back? Or sneak around and make sure Molly's there, then call the cops."

"You remember Ernie's Christine's brother, right? You're not going to get a lot of help from him," Spencer said, and I repeated for Jacy's benefit.

"Stealth mode it is."

Jacy drove along until we saw the farm, then looked for a spot to pull the ATV in out of sight.

"We aren't exactly dressed for this kind of thing. Should we have worn black and waited for it to get dark?"

Spencer faded out, I assumed to check if the coast was clear.

Jacy and I walked along through the tall grass beside the twin tracks left by ATVs until we stood across the road looking at the Murray farm. Spencer didn't come back, and now that we were there, I wasn't sure what to do.

"Well, she's not going to suspect anything if she sees me. I'll knock on the door and ask for help. I'll tell her the ATV broke down to create a distraction while you hunt around for Molly."

It wasn't much of a plan, but we went with it.

I crouched and stayed out of sight, crossed the road, and came up behind a small outbuilding on the right. From my hiding spot, I heard Jacy knock and spin her story, and Christine offer to call someone.

"It won't do any good. With all the yard sale madness, my husband's stuck at the house. It does this all the time, and I usually keep a wrench onboard, but it must have fallen out. Thanks for your time, but I can walk back to town."

I didn't have to see her face to know Jacy was giving Christine her best damsel in distress face. It was one of the ploys she'd perfected to get out of trouble when we were kids, and it worked so well she didn't even have to bring up her pregnancy.

"No, we have plenty of tools in the garage. Do you know what size you need?"

Their voices faded as the two women rounded the far corner of the house on the way to the garage. As soon as I was sure it was safe, I hurried toward the barn doing my best to maintain a balance between speed and silence.

The barn rose two stories high over a stacked stone foundation in the front that gave way to Y-shaped wooden piers in the back. The whole caper nearly fell through when a snake slithered out of the space between two stones, and I tried to jump sideways and run forward at the same time.

My feet tangled together, but I caught my balance before I face-planted, and then ducked around the corner. The cage was there, right where Spencer had said, and so was Molly. Above the tight leather muzzle, her eyes met mine, and the doggy version of hope flared to life.

Whining, because that was all the noise she could make, Molly pawed at the door, begging for release.

"Oh, my poor, sweet baby. What has she done? Did she hurt you?" I reached for the latch.

"Stop right there, Everly Dupree." Christine's voice came from several feet away and wouldn't have stopped me, except the next sound I heard was the ratcheting click-clack of a rifle being cocked to fire.

Not being a complete idiot, I stopped and turned to face the utter hardness on Christine Murray's face.

CHAPTER 23

"Where's Jacy? If you've hurt her I'll—"

"What? I'd like to hear you tell me what it is you think you'll do."

I had no weapon. Even if he could get out of town, Brian wouldn't come looking for us right away, no one else knew we were out here except Spencer, and he'd poofed off to wherever it is that ghosts go.

"Fine," I raised my hands in a show of surrender. "You're in charge, okay?"

"Damn right, I am. You thought you were so clever, but I knew you were lurking around somewhere as soon as I saw Jacy Wade at my door. Wherever one of you goes, the other can't be far behind. Well, you've lived in each other's pockets, so you might as well die that way."

"Can you at least tell me why? Why did you take Molly, and what did I ever do to you to make you want to kill me?" I asked partly to stall the inevitable, but mostly because I wanted to know.

"He should have gone to the pound and rescued a mutt. Not everyone has what it takes to raise a breeder." At first, her answer confused me, but then, in a flash, everything came clear.

"You killed Spencer." As soon as I said it, I realized I was right. "You killed him over Molly."

Christine's husband ran the paper shredder, so it made perfect sense that she might know the inner workings of the system.

"How did you get him to be in the right place at the right time?" The timing of it all had been the one thing I found hardest to reconcile.

In her cage, Molly began to circle. Three times to the left, then three times to the right, but I didn't dare take my eyes off Christine's face.

The rifle barrel lowered a fraction. "I didn't go there planning to kill him. That was just a happy accident. A twist of fate that let me put him down. Did you know he let that dog run wild? And did you know she's old enough to go into heat if she hasn't already. Spencer didn't care if she got bred by any old mutt. He didn't care that she shouldn't be bred until after her third heat at least."

Christine continued to spit venom. "He was the worst kind of owner. Imagine letting her play with tennis balls. Do you know what those things do to a dog's teeth? They're like chewing on sandpaper. I know how to take care of a dog like Molly. No one else will ever love her like I can."

Deja vu.

"I believe you." Humor her, my instincts screamed, but it didn't matter. Christine wanted to tell the story.

"I went over to talk to him. To see if I could get him to listen to reason. As usual, Molly was outside alone. Running loose. I coaxed her with some treats and snapped a leash on her. I figured I'd take her home, and keep her hidden for a few days. Then, if he showed up looking for her, I'd tell him she came to me, and offer to give him his money back for her."

Next time I saw Spencer, if there were a next time, I'd have to apologize to him for thinking he had the worst people skills on the planet. That honor belonged to Christine.

"But she barked her head off, and of course, he came running. He caught up to me at the recycling center, and the rest was easy. I wouldn't have hurt the dog, but he didn't know that. All I had to do was threaten her a little, and he stood right where I told him."

The woman was all kinds of twisted.

She described Spencer's death, in more detail than I wanted to hear. While she talked, I thought I caught a flutter of movement near the house.

"The dog went crazy, snapping at me, and lunging. Exhibiting the poor behavior that proved what a lousy owner he was. She bit the leash in half and took off. If you hadn't shown up for class, I probably would never have found her, but you did. Because Molly belongs with me."

For all she professed to love the dog, Christine paid almost no attention to Molly as she circled and circled. Spencer had to be close by, so why wasn't he doing anything to help me?

"Once you're gone, we'll be happy, won't we, Molly?"

Behind the muzzle, Molly growled.

Christine's lips firmed into a straight line.

"Now, we're going to take a little walk that way." She waved the barrel of the gun toward the road. "Turn around slowly, and don't make any sudden moves. I'd rather not have to shoot you before I throw you into the quarry, but I will if you make me."

"You don't have to do this, Christine. You're the best person to take care of Molly, I can see that now, and I won't give you any more trouble."

"Walk."

I struggled to force my body to fight its natural instincts and turn my back on the gun. Maybe Spencer had found a way to help Jacy, and that flutter of movement I'd seen was her getting out. I hoped so because it was too late to get help, and if one of us had to die, it should be me.

Cold and unyielding, the gun barrel pressed between my shoulder blades and left me no choice but to do as I was told, so I walked. Halfway between the barn and the road, a distinct chill swirled in from the right. It had to be Spencer, but I didn't dare turn my head to look.

"Jacy's pregnant, Christine," I said, hoping she'd show mercy. The constant pressure against my back eased, and we slowed to a stop. I thought I'd struck a nerve.

"I hope you haven't hurt the baby. You don't want an innocent life on your conscience, do you? Do whatever you want with me, but let Jacy and her baby go. She doesn't know anything about Spencer. I told her Molly probably came here because she prefers you to me. We just wanted to make sure she was safe. That's all Jacy knows. There's no reason to kill her."

When she didn't immediately prod me, I chanced a backward glance at Christine's face. Her attention focused on our right, and I realized I'd been wrong about hitting on her sympathy. She hadn't heard a word I said.

I shivered, partly out of fear, but partly because the gun barrel at my back had gone icy. Spencer's doing, I could only assume.

Did he think he if he made it cold enough, it wouldn't fire? I didn't know enough about guns to hazard a guess, but I figured it still would. I could see glimpses of the quarry through the trees. It

152

wouldn't be long now, and I'd follow Spencer when he passed through the veil. At least I'd solved his murder for him.

"Keep walking." If by some miracle, I survived this ordeal, I was going to have a huge bruise on my back. More likely, it would blend in with the rest as my body smashed against quarry stones on the way down.

I walked.

Across the road, across the ATV trail, and into the woods.

My body felt hollow, husked out.

I begged for my life, but couldn't shake Christine's resolve, and I finally fell silent to spend my last minutes thinking of family and wishing for a chance to say goodbye.

The shock of walking through Spencer's spectral presence brought me back to the present.

"Everly!" he shouted in my face. "Do you hear me?" I nodded slightly. "It's about time. Quit daydreaming and listen. When I give the word, I want you to drop to the ground and roll out of the way, okay?"

Nodding again, I allowed myself a flare of hope.

In another minute, Christine directed me to skirt a giant boulder, one of the many scattered throughout this part of the state by passing glaciers.

"Now!" Spencer shouted, and I forced my tense muscles to go limp.

I dropped like a stone and rolled left as Jacy shrieked, stepped out from behind the boulder, and brought a length of pipe down to knock the rifle out of Christine's hand. It landed right next to me, and since I had no idea how to use it, I grabbed it, and when I regained my feet, flung it into the quarry.

That done, I turned back to see Jacy and Christine engaged in battle. For all her gun-toting swagger, Christine fought like a girl. Jacy did not.

"That's for hitting me on the back of the head," Jacy growled as she landed a solid gut punch.

"This is for killing Spencer." An uppercut followed the gut punch.

A roundhouse kick took Christine down. "And that's for pointing a gun at my friend."

Breathing hard, Jacy turned to me. "Are you okay?"

153

"I am. Where'd you learn to fight like that?"

I never got to hear her answer. Dragging an out-of-breath Ernie Polk on the end of a leash, Molly raced through the woods toward us. She slathered my face with kisses as soon as I removed the muzzle.

Ernie stared down at his sister, then turned his gaze on me. "What happened here?"

We told him. Christine admitted everything, and I felt bad for Ernie when, with gentle hands, he had to put cuffs on his own sister. He didn't say much, but he didn't need to; the grave expression on his face did all the talking.

With Ernie following behind, Jacy went off to the hospital in an ambulance to be checked for a concussion. We would both go to the station to make our official statements the next day, and that left Molly and me to ride the ATV back to town—a trip that took considerably longer since I had a lot to think about.

I hadn't seen Spencer since he told me to drop, but I knew he wouldn't leave without saying goodbye to his dog, and I was right. About halfway back, he popped into the back seat. Molly tried her spinning routine, and I almost caused us to have an accident trying to stop to avoid her falling out.

"Don't take this the wrong way, but I'll be glad when you're gone," I told him.

"Won't be long now. I just wanted to thank you for everything. Especially for taking care of Molly. I know you're going to be good with her."

On that point, I could reassure him. "I love her, and while I doubt she'll forget you, I'll do my best to give her a happy home. Hey, can you tell me how Jacy managed to get ahead of us? I figure you had something to do with that."

"I had everything to do with it." Arrogant as always. "She was down when I found her, and I remembered how you said I made things cold, so I stuck my hand on the bump to help bring down the swelling and wake her up. That took a minute. She's a feisty one, though. Came up off the floor ready to fight."

"She would."

"It was sheer luck that Polk was already on this side of town when she called him."

Luck or serendipity. Lately, I couldn't always tell one from the other.

"How did you get her to follow you?"

Grinning, Spencer said, "That was a stroke of genius on my part. Jacy figured out I was there pretty fast once I poked her a few times, and she made it outside in time to hear Christine say she was going to throw you into the quarry. I guided her into place by touching her left or right hand."

"Well, it worked, so I guess we're even now."

Because we were, it was time for Spencer to go into the light. He said goodbye to Molly and I swear she understood this was their last moment together, because she whined and looked at me with sad eyes. When he was gone, I hugged her, and maybe I cried a little. She'll never tell, and neither will I.

The yard sale was winding down when I drove home, but I was too tired to care that I'd missed my chance at making some extra cash. All I wanted was my house and my dog. With her head resting on my leg, Molly seemed to agree.

Though I hadn't started the week wanting a dog, I couldn't imagine now what I'd ever do without her. It seemed both of us had found a home.

Made in the USA
Las Vegas, NV
23 February 2021